KU-066-607

A STRANGE INHERITANCE

Everybody dreams of a surprise inheritance . . . Meg is at her lowest ebb when she finds that her uncle, Henry Waterston — who she never even knew existed — has left her a derelict windmill in a Yorkshire dale. With the gift comes a strange final request, asking her to 'help close the circle'. Meg visits the mill, falls in love with the place and throws herself into the challenge of rebuilding the old business. In the process she finds new friends — and a new love. But who exactly was Henry Waterston, and why did he leave Meg everything he owned?

Books by Mark Neilson
Published by The House of Ulverscroft:

THE VALLEY OF THE VINES

MARK NEILSON

◆

A STRANGE INHERITANCE

Complete and Unabridged

ULVERSCROFT
Leicester

First published in Great Britain in 2012 by
Robert Hale Limited
London

First Large Print Edition
published 2013
by arrangement with
Robert Hale Limited
London

The moral right of the author has been asserted

Copyright © 2012 by Mark Neilson
All rights reserved

A catalogue record for this book is available
from the British Library.

ISBN 978–1–4448–1572–6

Published by
F. A. Thorpe (Publishing)
Anstey, Leicestershire

Set by Words & Graphics Ltd.
Anstey, Leicestershire
Printed and bound in Great Britain by
T. J. International Ltd., Padstow, Cornwall

This book is printed on acid-free paper

*To the cherished memory
of our son, Mark*

Acknowledgements

It is impossible to research the background for any novel without knocking on the doors of many busy people and asking questions that must drive them mad. Equally, in the process of writing, others get asked for an opinion, or have their best ideas stolen without a second thought or even a hint of compensation.

To everyone who took the time to help me, I would like to convey my heartfelt thanks. Any mistakes remaining in this novel are down to me, as writer, and not the responsibility of those who tried to keep me right.

In particular, I would like to thank Fionn my tame(ish) Conservation Officer, for talking me through what must and can be done to listed buildings, to qualify as acceptable remedial work. Likewise Jim, my veteran baker: yes, I know you don't come from anywhere near Yorkshire and that you're nobbut a lad — but I stole you and your ideas nevertheless. And Lyn and Diane, who stoically read bits of the story and fed back (mostly) encouragement. To Alan and Tracey, who are both editors and friends, thanks for your suggestion when

I was racking my brains in vain: your football team will one day rise from the ashes, I hope — so long as we can still beat them.

Penultimate thanks are due to my long suffering wife. Now that the book is finished, I will certainly get down to all the gardening and the painting that is needed — unless another idea comes up and taps me on the shoulder . . .

Finally, I would like to thank all my friends in Kirkbymoorside, and whatever quirk of genetic programming that allows Yorkshiremen to smile, occasionally. Too often would get boring. I love their countryside, and some of its residents are OK too. If you buy the first round, while they are still searching deep inside their pockets, that is . . .

1

Seagulls wheeled and called above the urban parkland, but Megan Waterston neither saw nor heard them. In crisp Edinburgh sunshine, she was walking slowly along the path which cut across The Meadows, head down and deep in thought.

She should never have done it, she brooded. Given in to her instinct of disgust, and been so outspoken. Right or wrong, it had cost her a job which she had worked eight long years to make her own. Meg frowned, stopping to kick a stick across the path: if she had bitten her tongue she would have condoned her boss's milking great chunks of personal money from an engineering business which was struggling to stay afloat. She would have become one of them, the managers who mindlessly lined their pockets with every allowance they could claim or steal, when they were already drawing down more than four times her own salary.

Meg stared at the well-chewed stick and sighed. Instead, she had challenged the man for whom she worked — and lost her job as his hard-working personal assistant, despite the fact that she did half his job for him. While the other managers turned and looked away, guilty of fiddling their own expenses even more frenziedly than Nero had fiddled while Rome burned to the ground.

Thieves hang together, if exposing one exposes all.

Into her arc of vision came a small ragged dog, which pounced on the stick she had kicked away and brought it back to her feet. Then it looked up, bright eyes shining through ragged hair as it wagged its tail.

'Not today.' Meg smiled.

It was impossible to feel depressed in front of that small face.

The dog picked up the stick and carried it closer still, dropping it across the toes of her shoes. More frenzied tail-wagging.

'Fritz!' Meg heard a woman's voice. She looked up to see a small woman, dressed in flamboyant grey and purple ethnic clothes, with the same sort of fly-away hair as the dog, scurrying across The Meadows towards her. 'I'm so sorry,' the woman panted. 'He's obsessed with twigging . . . '

'Twigging? Pardon?'

'Bringing twigs for you to throw. He's a very naughty boy.' The woman smiled down indulgently.

'Not a problem,' said Meg.

She stepped around the dog, who picked up the stick and followed her, setting it down in front of her again and giving one single high-pitched yip. The sound of a dog accustomed to getting its own way. A command, almost.

'He likes you,' the woman said. 'He's always finding doggy people. Here, I'll throw his ball. That usually gets his attention.' She threw the yellow tennis ball with all her might — but absolutely no control. The ball flashed past Meg's face. 'Fetch!' the woman called.

The small dog hesitated, torn between ball and stick. Finally he solved the dilemma by picking up the stick and chasing after the ball, with the stick in his mouth. While Meg beat a hasty retreat — as much from the owner as her dog.

However, the chance encounter left her smiling. So what; she was out of work — and out of luck in applying for other jobs as a PA anywhere. Not a good time to be looking for work, but something would turn up. At least she wasn't trapped in an airless office, glimpsing the sunshine through double-glazed glass. She was out and walking in it, feeling the wind stir her hair. Unconsciously, she swept her dark hair back with her fingers.

Time to get back to her flat and start using her laptop to see what she could find on the job market. There had to be some big business, somewhere, looking for a hard working and loyal PA. Or any work that brought in a wage.

Meg walked briskly through the lines of up-market flats, into the hinterland where ordinary people lived. She found herself enjoying the exercise, singing as she walked. Maybe she should be looking for some sort of work in the open air — but what? She smiled, searching through her bag for her door key. A female lumberjack? A traffic warden, choking in exhaust fumes all day long? A deck-chair attendant? Lollipop lady? There had to be something waiting for her.

As she opened the door, it scraped over the day's post. Including a single white and expensive-looking envelope, on which her name and address were neatly typed. Probably another bill — they seemed to sense when money was tight, and arrived in flocks on her doorstep. But why waste a good envelope on a bill?

Intrigued, Meg threw her jacket across a chair and walked easily over to her flat's windows. She hesitated, then eased a finger inside the flap and pulled it gently free. Inside was an even crisper sheet of headed business paper.

Meg slid this out, opened it properly, and

skimmed through the short contents. She frowned, reading the letter a second time. Glancing at the address, she shook her head in puzzlement.

It was a lawyer's letter — not a scam, from what she could see and sense. A sober, careful note, asking her to phone the partnership's number and arrange to travel down to a London office in Haymarket, bringing with her some proof of identity: a driving licence, and/or passport, and a utilities bill or bank statement, sent to her at her present address.

Proof of identity? Meg smiled wryly. Just now, out of work and depressed, she wasn't too sure who or what she was. Just another, invisible, member of the army of Scottish unemployed. But she had her licence, passport, and bills to spare — most of them paid.

She read through the letter again. Any reasonable expenses incurred by you would be reimbursed. Did 'reasonable' stretch to flying? Business class, then staying overnight at the Ritz? Behaving just like her erstwhile boss would have done? Or should she play it safe, travel down by overnight express coach, to save B and B — just in case it was all a joke? No, she would ask them on the phone, and make sure that whatever she did would be covered. She hadn't enough money left to be cavalier.

But why should a London lawyer have got so soberly in touch with her?

Before she phoned, she had better get her head round what she needed to know. On automatic pilot, she reached for her diary, to check when she was free then the ridiculousness of the situation got to her and she began to laugh. With exaggerated care she went through the pages of her diary. They were all blank.

'At least, I won't be double-booked,' she thought.

She walked over to the flat's window and looked down, unseeing, at the steady stream of traffic below, and the busy pavement. A mystery lawyer and a mystery letter. Was it the usual cliché, that she might learn something to her advantage — or was it, maybe, the reverse?

She keyed the office number into her mobile phone, and dialled. Only one way to find out.

In any case, what did she have to lose?

★　★　★

Jo Chisholm leaned wearily on the tailgate of her old estate car before bracing herself and hauling out the last plastic crate of her baking. It was still predawn and, in the slowly greying dark, she walked through the muffled-up figures of the stallholders setting up their stalls for the weekly market day in Kirkbymoorside. Several of the figures nodded to her, regulars acknowledging another regular, and she grunted back. The last crate was always heavier than the rest.

Jo shook her head impatiently. Yes, she was hurting — but so was everybody else in this predawn gloom. Nobody set up and ran a market stall simply for the love of it. It was hard relentless work, moving from country town to country town around the North Yorkshire moors, staying resolutely brash and cheerful, and selling at a slender margin to make some sort of a living. People only went to markets when they were looking for bargains — and hard-nosed Yorkshire people would bargain down the price of a scone. If you let them.

With a tired grunt, Jo lifted the crate a little higher and dumped it on the bare boards of a stall. 'That's it, Phil,' she said. 'Where's my money? I have to get back home and put the kids out to school.'

The cold, pinched face of the stallholder broke into a smile. 'Haway, lass,' he said. 'Tha's far too young for kids. Still in t' full bloom of youth.'

'If only.'

'Then change your mirror. That's how you look to me.'

'Flattery received and acknowledged — but you should have gone to Specsavers.'

'What? When I can buy glasses for fiver in t'market?' Phil smiled. 'What do I owe thee then — the usual?'

'A dozen big cakes, assorted. Two dozen jam-sandwich sponges. Two dozen ginger-breads. Four dozen scones, and pancakes. All wrapped up.'

'Right. That's twenty-four pounds for cakes, twenty pounds each for jam sandwiches and gingers, six pounds each for scones and pan-cakes . . . ' Phil drew a wad of notes from the hip pocket of his jeans and began to count. 'I've no change yet,' he said. 'Here's seventy-five pounds.'

'Then you still owe me one pound.'

'Nowt wrong with your arithmetic.' He chuck-led, reaching deep into his jeans' side pocket and sifting through loose change. 'Here. These cakes o' yours go like snow in t' summer. No chance you can do an extra dozen jam-sandwich rolls and gingers — even another couple of dozen scones and pancakes?'

'On an ordinary kitchen cooker? You must be joking.'

'There were no harm in asking. See you on Friday again?'

Jo shuddered. Friday was the Helmsley market, another twenty minutes away from home and an even earlier rise. 'Right,' she said.

'Be good.'

'No chance to be anything else.'

Phil grinned. 'You never know . . . if I finish early . . . '

'You'll find the front door locked, and a couple of Rottweillers at the back.'

'Sounds like a right good Yorkshire welcome.'

Jo smiled. 'Take care, Phil,' she said.

'You too, lass.'

There was proper light in the sky now, as the busy figures bolted iron frames, set wooden trestles and began to unload their wares and set them out on display. Dirty Ford Transits sat parked at the back of each stall, rear doors wide open. Jo edged through the hard-working figures and walked down the broad main street towards her own car. She threw herself inside and counted the money: not much, for two days' work — when you took off the cost of the ingredients and packaging, then the time and effort of repeated baking in a hot kitchen.

She grimaced. She had no idea of what she was paying herself to work, but she needed the money to fill the chasm left in her family's finances after the pitiful MOD's widow's pension had been spent. Jim would never have wanted this, but you have no choice when you find the landmine with your name on it. Fighting a war which had little logic and had now cost 300 British soldiers' lives — all for a corrupt government and a tribal people who didn't want democracy.

Her car refused to start. Ruthlessly, she tried again, and a third time, before the engine fired. It needed servicing. Her whole life and house needed servicing, and a bit of TLC. But there was no time. There were kids to haul out of bed, then their breakfast to get ready while she kept an eye on them to make sure they were washing and dressing and not daydreaming, then make sure they ate enough to last them through to lunchtime, then the run with them down from Fadmoor to pick up their local school bus services.

After all that she could sit down for an exhausted cup of tea. Twenty minutes, maximum, before she had to climb into her car again, and head off to start her other job, which was walking rich people's dogs. There were times when she felt like a tame mouse running on a treadmill. But there was a difference, both in size and in intent. The mouse was only playing, to fill in its time. While for Jo there was no choice. Because there was nobody else to earn, to feed her family.

No one other than herself.

★　★　★

'Come in, please.'

Meg stepped past the smartly dressed secretary, who had led her to the senior partner's office, and went towards the figure rising from behind his desk.

'Hello, I'm Robert Matthews. Please sit down, Miss Waterston . . . no, not in front of the desk, that's too formal. Let's make ourselves comfortable. Would you like a coffee?'

'Yes, please.'

Meg found herself gently ushered into a corner of the office, where comfortable old leather armchairs faced each other over a low glass table. The man's handshake had been firm, but not too firm. His hand warm, not cold or clammy. The senior partner of the legal firm was tall and slim, in his early fifties she guessed, and with white wings of hair at both temples, giving him gravitas.

He sat down opposite her, his grey eyes watchful but a slight smile on his face. 'Did you have a pleasant trip down?' he asked politely.

Meg smiled. 'That's the first time I've travelled on business class.'

The smile became a conspiratorial grin. 'It's the only place where there's enough space for my legs when I'm flying,' he said. 'That's my excuse.'

Meg found herself liking the man. He wasn't stuffy at all, as she had expected. She reached into her bag, brought out the proof of identity and pushed the papers across the glass table towards him. He touched them with his hand in acknowledgement while maintaining eye contact.

'I hate London,' she found herself saying. 'It's always so busy, and so noisy. People pushing past you. Buses, traffic fumes. Edinburgh's bad, but we usually have a brisk wind to blow the fumes away. They hang in the air here.'

'A real Londoner would get drunk on fresh air.' He smiled.

The coffee came through: delicate porcelain cups on an immaculate tray, with an old silver coffee pot.

'Shall I be mother?' he asked, reaching forward without waiting for an answer. She studied his hands, as he lifted out the cups and poured. Long sensitive fingers, crisp white shirt, no cufflinks. Then he was handing over a cup of coffee to her; the aroma was delicious.

Meg sipped. The taste was as good as the smell. No instant coffee, this.

Matthews poured, then set aside his own cup and saucer. He picked up the proof of identity, opened her passport and glanced across at her, then flicked through the array of bills she had brought. Then, he nodded and pushed the paperwork back across the desk to her. 'I think we can take it from these that you really are Megan Waterston.'

'I hope so.' Meg found herself responding to the friendly smile. 'Now, could you put me out of my misery, please? Why do you want to see me? I can't, for the life of me, think what it could be.'

Matthews slowly ran long fingers through his hair. 'Have you heard of Henry Waterston?' he asked.

Meg blinked. 'No. Never. What about him?'

Matthews stroked his chin with a long index finger. 'It seems he was your uncle,' he said quietly. 'Your father's brother.'

'I didn't even know that my father had a brother.'

'I understand, from our research, that there was some deep dispute. The two brothers split up, and never contacted each other again.'

Meg frowned. 'I honestly can't remember my mother or father ever mentioning his name, while they were still alive.'

'Family disputes can sometimes end like that, in a complete refusal to acknowledge the existence of each other. If you have never heard of Henry Waterston, then you shouldn't be too upset to know that he recently died.'

'I'm sorry,' Meg said automatically.

Matthews nodded in acknowledgement. 'We are entrusted, as executors, to wind up and disperse Henry Waterston's estate. Many years ago Mr Waterston sat exactly where you are sitting now, and dictated his instructions for his last will and testament to me. Obviously, we set these intentions in legal terms. But his wishes were simple and were never changed over the intervening years. He named you, Megan Waterston, daughter of Thomas Waterston, as the sole beneficiary to his estate.'

Meg shook her head. 'That was my father's name — but I have still never heard of, or know, a Henry Waterston . . . '

Matthews smiled. 'The crucial point is that he appeared to know you.'

He rose smoothly from the low armchair and went over to his desk, then returned with a few sheets of paper and a long white envelope in his hands. 'I can read through the legal phrases for you,' he said gently. 'Or cut to the chase, as we say nowadays, and tell you

14

what your position and inheritance are.'

'Tell me, please — as simply as possible.'

Matthews nodded. 'With no other benefi-ciaries, there is no need to be excessively formal. Henry Waterston left you the major portion of the property he owned, the Valley Mill, near a market town called Kirkbymoor-side. That's at the southern edge of the North Yorkshire moors. His instructions were to sell his London flat and use the proceeds from that to settle all his debts. The residual amount, after taxes, is the balance of his estate, and also yours.'

Meg's heart was racing, her mind almost locked in the confusion of thoughts which exploded through it. This couldn't be true — it must be a dream.

'How much?' she asked faintly, her voice coming out as almost a croak.

'The mill and three hundred and ninety-five thousand pounds, give or take a few pounds. The statement of settlement is here.' Matthews pushed the document across the glass table-top.

Meg looked at it blindly. 'There surely must be a mistake?' she said, sliding it back to him. 'I've never heard of the man. This has to be a case of mistaken identity.'

'As our football crowds are fond of chanting, there is only one Megan Waterston.

We have already checked, when we were tracing you.'

'But why?'

Matthews slowly folded the legal documents and set them down on the table. 'Our job, as lawyers, is to carry out our client's instructions. Not to quiz him — or her — on why these instructions have been given. All I can tell you is that Henry Waterston was deeply moved, when he dictated the terms of his will. He was a big, gruff man — yet he had to stop several times to blow his nose and wipe his eyes. That is the one and only time I ever met him, but the obvious depth of his emotion made a huge impression. Whether you knew him or not, he knew you. I can still see the pain and yearning on his face. I remember waiting to see if he would explain things to me, but as soon as he had finished, Waterston rose and told me to send him our bill, along with the unsigned will when it was ready.'

The calm grey eyes were very direct. 'Perhaps he has left an explanation here,' Matthews continued. He slid the white envelope across the table-top.

Meg picked it up. Her name was written on it, in a square strong hand.

Beneath her name, the legend: *To be opened in the event of my death.*

She stared at the script.

'You may choose to open it on your own,' Matthews said gently. 'I am happy to leave you alone in my office for a few minutes.'

Meg shook her head. 'No need,' she said.

Matthews sat patiently, while Meg plucked up the courage to open the envelope. After some moments, she tried with shaking hands to ease up the flap of the envelope but the edge was stuck firmly down.

Matthews crossed to his desk, then came back.

'Try this,' he said, offering her a long slim paper-knife.

In the quiet office the sound of its blade cutting paper seemed very loud.

Meg hesitated again, then eased out the single sheet of notepaper, on which there was the same blunt handwriting. She read it, then handed it wordlessly to the lawyer. 'Have you any idea what this means?' she asked hoarsely.

Matthews took the letter, read it swiftly, and handed it back.

'The letter has been lying in our safe for years. I never knew its contents.'

Meg looked down at the short note again, her eyes blurring with tears. Even if she didn't know the man from Adam, and hadn't the faintest idea of what the words meant, there was something in the simple message which touched her heart.

Meg, lassie, you were dearly loved by someone you never knew. I am trusting this will close the circle, and help me Rest in Peace. Henry Waterston.

'What on earth does he mean?' she asked.

★　★　★

Deep within the dale and its thick woods Jo always felt that she could have been walking through wilderness territory because all sounds from the town and the moorland road were muffled. She liked the feeling of being on her own, out in the wilds. The trees brought their own sense of peace and calm — something she craved in the endless hurly-burly of her life.

At a gap in the trees she halted. The golden pine needles on the forest floor in front of her had been disturbed. A deer had been raking with a front hoof, looking for grubs.

'Come here, Ben!' she called.

Reluctantly, the old Labrador trotted back to her, looking longingly into the woods with his muzzle twitching. He could smell the scent of deer more clearly than she could see their traces. And any dog, no matter how old, forgets its owner when in hot pursuit of a quarry which is engrained in its genes.

Jo clipped the leash on to his collar. Better safe than sorry — not least because she simply hadn't enough time in her day to chase after someone else's dog that had bolted. 'Come on, boy,' she said. 'Let's go down to the river.'

The path down to the riverbank was an old and overgrown track. It meant a shorter walk than Jo had planned, but it took her to one of her favourite places in the world — and guided them both away from the deer traces. Humming, she walked briskly down the track as it wound through the conifers into the native woodland above the riverbank. The sound of running water became ever stronger as she dropped down to the valley floor.

The track emerged at the side of an ancient ford, now long disused and almost forgotten. On the far bank of the river there was an old yellow Yorkshire sandstone building, fallen into minor disrepair. Some windows were boarded, some were broken, all were filthy from the dirt of ages. Moss grew on the wide slates of its roof, and hung from the sides of an ancient millwheel.

Jo found a trunk of a fallen tree upon which to sit and admire the view. Around her was ancient woodland. Above the high canopy of tree branches and fresh green leaves white clouds slipped across a blue sky. There was a wonderful sense of peace around the old mill, a silence accentuated rather than broken by the sound of a gentle breeze through the trees, and the cooing of a wood pigeon.

This was as close to heaven as she could get, Jo thought contentedly. Down here she could dream that she was back in her native Scottish Borders, a slim girl who had yet to meet the love of her life, an indestructible soldier who would become an indestructible sergeant major, looking after his boys with a will of iron and holding them safe in his grip.

Until Death got tired of his defiance, and had killed him outright, bringing to an end the only life Jo had ever wanted, or had ever known.

She sniffed. Jim and she had done much of their courting in a forest glade like this. Holding hands and staring out across a Borders river and dreaming of the children they would have, and the home they would make. Planning for the career Jim would have to find when the Royal Scottish Borderers were finished with him and he was pensioned off. They had never planned for death. Back in those days, death was something that scarcely ever happened and, when it did, it happened to other people.

At her feet the old dog whimpered in his sleep, bringing her back to the present and its pain.

'Come on, fella,' she said, reaching down to smooth the golden hair. 'Let's get you back to your home and your dinner.'

A quick glance at her watch confirmed what she expected: she was running late, and had better rush the old dog home, then get down to the bus stop in Kirkby, to pick up the younger of her two children.

Jo sighed. No rest for the wicked — and judging by the little rest she got, she must have been pretty bad. The thought cheered her up. She was a fighter, a survivor, and no matter how bad she felt inside she would die before she quit. She reached down and unclipped the old dog.

'Race you to your dinner dish,' she challenged.

Then set off at a trot, back up the mossy track.

★ ★ ★

'Well, Miss Waterston, have you slept on it?' Robert Matthews rose courteously from his desk and came over to shake Meg's hand and guide her towards the comfortable chairs.

She grimaced. 'I couldn't sleep on anything

last night,' she said. 'I was too excited and confused. I still think it's a case of mistaken identity — and, anyway, call me Meg . . . everybody does.'

Matthews smiled. He liked this direct young Scotswoman.

'No mistake,' he said briskly. 'We checked you out thoroughly, once we had traced you. If you haven't slept, would you like some coffee?'

'Yes, please.' Meg scrubbed her eyes, which felt full of sand. 'Tell me, have you read all these books around your office?' She gestured to the shelves which were bending beneath the weight of legal tomes, the most elderly and frayed of which lived behind the glass of an equally ancient cabinet.

Matthews closed his office door and grinned. It took years off his face.

'My old dad used to say that we lawyers charged by the yard of the books on our shelves,' he said with a laugh. 'Then he used to add that if we charged by the thickness of his football season ticket — he was a dedicated West Ham supporter — we would still be charging far too much. Yes, I do dip into them when I'm searching for case precedent. In a sense, they are a fairly complete record of key cases over the last hundred and fifty years. But if I had to put my hand on my heart, it would be to admit that some of them have never been opened in my lifetime.'

The secretary brought in the immaculate tray for coffee.

'Help yourself to biscuits,' Matthews said, pouring for both of them.

'I might spray crumbs.'

'Then let us both feel free to do that.'

Matthews studied Meg's face. There were dark shadows under her eyes.

'What's your thinking, anyway?' he asked. 'Do you want to keep the old mill, or put the property on to the market and convert it into financial capital.'

Meg tried, for the millionth time since she had heard of her strange inheritance, to think both logically and clearly. And failed, yet again.

'I don't know,' she said simply. 'What would you advise?'

'Oh dear,' said Matthews. 'It's never easy, as an objective outsider, to judge what the client will want to hear, and what might give offence.'

'I don't offend easily. It's an objective view I need.'

'Very well.' Matthews sat back in his armchair, holding his coffee cup absent-mindedly, cupped in both hands. That simple action made him seem more human and caring, somehow. 'On balance, I think you should sell,' he said slowly. 'An old disused mill, by definition, is going to be in a state of some disrepair — there could be rampant damp and possibly even rot, coming both from the weather and its near-water location. Construction work costs a fortune, these days. It's as if builders don't want the work, and charge a crazy price to put you off, thinking that if you're daft enough to accept their estimate, then it's really worth their time. So, to keep the property, you must factor in a huge bill for remedial work — quite possibly in six figures, and that's not including the pence!'

For a moment, a smile flickered on his serious face. 'Now, if you sell, what would be the selling points in its favour? Firstly, properties along the foot of the moors are very desirable, both for retirement and, don't be surprised, for commuting down the fast rail link through York to London. Secondly, since we would be aiming at people with enough money for any conversion work, quirky properties often carry a premium price. Let someone with money to burn pay for the rebuilding. Thirdly, I would have to research this, but it may be that your old mill is subject to a conservation order — in which case, negotiating permission to do anything could involve months of hassle. Once again, better to leave that to someone who can pay people like us to do the hassling for them.'

Matthews sighed, and paused to take a slow sip of coffee. 'Therefore, my advice would be to avoid taking on what might be a major nightmare, and place it on the market for others to fight over. Having said that, I should warn you that interest rates are minimal on capital sums today. So you might well get a better return by holding the property for a few years. But, on balance, I would still sell — and pass the risks on to someone else.' He smiled. 'No offence, I hope?'

'None taken.' Meg sipped the wonderful coffee, feeling herself slowly come to life again. 'That's more or less what I have been saying to myself all night. But the second I decide to do as you say, I find myself backing away. If I sell, I am letting down an uncle whom I never saw — a man whom I didn't even know existed. There is something in his letter that touches my heart. He's pleading for something — is it for me to try and put the mill to rights again? Or is he talking about something I don't understand, some link between the two of us?'

A silence settled in the lawyer's office. Outside, the hum of London's traffic seemed far away — almost in another world.

'There is no need to rush through a decision,' Matthews said at last. 'Why not go home to Edinburgh and think about it up there, once you have come more to terms with your inheritance? Decide in haste, repent at leisure.' That warm smile flashed again. 'That isn't quite a legal quotation, but lawyers make a very comfortable living trying to extract people and businesses from decisions which have been made with undue haste. So, in advising you to take your time, I am acting against the interests of my profession.'

'Appreciated.' Meg smiled.

The small antique clock on the office wall chimed the half-hour, in discreet but expensive tones.

'Do you know what?' Meg said slowly.

Matthews inclined his head, waiting.

It was an impulse, a crazy impulse. But now that she was a rich woman she could afford the odd impulse or two. So long as they didn't cost too much.

'I've just decided,' Meg said.

'To sell?'

'Not yet. I am going to take the train back to York. Then I'm going to hire a small car and drive up to Kirkbymoorside — what a lovely name. I'm going to book in for a few nights B and B there, in a decent old hotel.

Then I'm going to wander round the place. It's an area that I've never seen before. And, while I'm there, I am going to search for that old mill building . . . what did you say it was called?'

'The Valley Mill. Yorkshire folk don't waste time on fancy names.'

'Then I'm going to visit the Valley Mill, take my time and look around the place with an open mind. I'll decide what to do with it once I'm standing in the property that Henry Waterston left me. It's the very least I can do for him, by way of saying 'thanks'.'

'An admirable decision,' Matthews said with a smile.

Now that the choice was made Meg was suddenly full of energy. She stood up and held out her hand. 'Thank you, for your help and advice,' she said. 'I understand that English law is quite different from the law we have in Scotland?'

Matthews nodded. 'You take your legal base from Roman and French law — ours has come from different and more complex sources.'

'Therefore I will need an English lawyer to act for me in this?'

'Indeed. I can recommend several excellent solicitors, who will come much cheaper than myself . . . ' Matthews gestured to the groaning shelves. 'It's the yardage of books, you know.' He smiled.

'I would prefer you. I trust you.'

'Thank you. Then I would be happy to act for you.'

Meg reached out and shook the firm hand. 'I will keep you in the picture,' she promised. 'And I will phone you to talk through what I am doing, before I finally make up my mind and do it.'

'Best of luck.'

From his office window Matthews watched her trim figure walk quickly through the stream of pedestrians. He watched until he could no longer see the dark head and the erect shoulders. There was so much about this young woman that reminded him of his wife, although the two women were poles apart in both appearance and background. Something about Meg's sense of humour, her direct and independent mind, and her self deprecation made him draw the comparison.

He sighed, and went thoughtfully back to his desk.

In the street below Meg walked through the canyons of tall buildings, chopping and changing her stride pattern to avoid people who had no intention of avoiding her. This had to be the rudest and most uncaring city in the world — as well as the dirtiest. A puff of wind blew grit into her face, made her stop and try to wipe her eyes.

She blinked through the tears of discomfort. So that was it — as quickly as it had taken for that old clock to chime in Robert Matthews's office she had set the course of action that she would follow over the next two weeks or so. She would splash out some money on herself — but not too much — and treat herself to an unplanned holiday. Then she would search for a mill that could be a crumbling pile of stones, and make a token gesture towards the shadow of a man she had never known. A man who had made her a new woman with no need to work, who had left her rich. Although money had never been important to her, so long as she had enough to do what she wanted, whenever the casual notion took a more serious form.

Meg set off again, driven by the same surge of restless energy that had come from nowhere in the lawyer's office. She liked that man; she would trust him to help her to do whatever she decided. In the meantime . . . She looked up at the patch of grey sky framed by the tall buildings around her.

The sooner she shook the dust of London from her feet and escaped to North Yorkshire the better, she thought.

2

Meg Waterston looked down the lines of busy market stalls in Pickering. Market day at the edge of the North Yorkshire moors brought everybody in from the dales, which cut deep into the moorland. The brightly coloured stalls sold everything, from farmers' boots to dancing shoes, from heavy-duty anoraks to the latest tops and handbags, from local butchers' meat to home-made bread and cakes.

She had walked slowly up one side of the main street, edging round the bargaining, jostled by farmers' wives and tourists. This country market had an air of vibrancy that you never got in cities. And above it all, a brisk Yorkshire wind blew white clouds across a clear blue sky.

Meg instinctively loved the place and drank in the air of busy excitement as if it were sparkling wine. She had driven over from Kirkbymoorside, simply to fill in her morning and get a feel for the rolling green countryside.

In the bright sunlight she ambled down the other side of a street, stepping aside to let a local woman climb into a muddy white van to try on jeans from someone's stall; on market days it seemed Ford Transits were the unisex changing-rooms. No careful counting of clothing items here: you climbed in with an armful of clothes draped over your arm, struggled in partial privacy to try things on, then came out and threw the unwanted clothes back on to the stall and set about the serious business of trying to shave more money off the price of the chosen items.

'You'll pay twelve pounds for this top in Next,' a trader told Meg. 'I'll give it to you for three pounds. Or seven pounds for three — even if that means taking the bread from my family's mouth. Coom on, lass, can you afford to turn the offer down?'

'No thanks.' Meg smiled.

'How about . . . ' the trader turned to rummage among the jackets hanging at the back of the stall, then found that she had disappeared. Not put out in the slightest, he grabbed another top and started his sales pitch on someone else.

'Over in Helmsley, there's a man that has three feet,' another stall holder earnestly told the watching crowd. 'He always comes here to buy his shoes . . . the best prices and quality in Yorkshire.'

'Haway! What does he do with t'spare shoe?' a local bantered back.

'Simple! He gives it to his brother — for he has three feet too.'

'Yer shoes are like yer jokes, lad. They're rubbish!'

Meg laughed outright. Then she found the stallholder's eyes locked on to her, twinkling. 'I have just t'pair of shoes for you, my lass,' he continued seamlessly.

'No thanks,' said Meg.

'Princess Anne tried them on, in Halifax?'

'She mun ha' been wanting t' get out of rain,' a local farmwife commented.

Clearly, market days were for entertainment as much as filling your cupboards. All done in high good humour. Meg ambled slowly down the street until she ran out of stalls. A second lap? She checked her watch: no, better find a place to eat. A café, maybe? Or buy a pie, a sandwich, or a cake. What about that stall near the church, where the baking had looked just like home baking?

Meg hesitated. It was too nice a day to go into a hotel or café — and the tables would be thronged, in any case. Although it was something she seldom did, she fancied dining alfresco in a park, here, or back in Kirkbymoorside. She headed back up the busy street.

How could she be hungry, having eaten the largest breakfast in her life? It must be the

Yorkshire air — or the sheer joy of living. Meg pushed in to the edge of the cake stall. A gorgeous-looking pork pie caught her attention; it was carved into wedges that would stop a ploughman in his tracks. Meg pointed, and bought. 'And could I have a single scone?' she asked.

'A single scone — or a dozen, lass. They were made by a Scotswoman, just like thee. Want butter on't?'

Meg hesitated, then abandoned caution.

'Please. How did you guess I was Scottish?'

'With an accent like that, no need to guess . . . '

Meg retreated, clutching her lunch. Where best to eat it, in this thronged market town? She followed her nose, and found herself in a lane which ran alongside a stream. Under its trees, she sat on a low wall, and took a bite at her pie. Unbelievable. She wiped crumbs from her face. If she stayed here much longer, she would be putting on weight. As she took another huge bite, a blackbird settled on a branch above the stream and began to sing — with one beady eye fixed on her picnic. Meg broke off a corner of the pastry crust.

The song ended abruptly, as the blackbird pounced.

After she finished her lunch, Meg thought, she would drive back to her hotel and ask where to find the old Valley Mill. Left to her by a man she didn't know, but who had transformed her life by his kindness. Going up to look at the old building was the least she could do.

Before she sold the place.

* * *

Jo Chisholm checked her watch. She was on schedule, starting her fourth dogwalk of the day, with the ancient Labrador Ben. He plodded stolidly in front of her, refusing to acknowledge that any smells were worthy of his attention on the cobbled street. Ben was a creature of habit, only coming to life when she reached the woods and slipped his leash. Up there, all sorts of furry creatures had left their calling cards, so that even an aged Labrador could sniff ecstatically, remembering the days when he could give anything a chase for its money.

'Excuse me?'

Jo turned. A young dark-haired woman was walking towards her and, from two words spoken, she already recognized a fellow Scot, as rare as hen's teeth down here, where Yorkshire and London mixed.

'Yes?' she said.

'I'm looking for the Valley Mill. Somebody

34

told me it was up at the top of the town, past the brass band practice hut — but I can't find that either.'

Jo smiled. 'It's a silver band,' she said. 'The track you're looking for is further up the Fadmoor road. But you can reach the mill from here. There's another track through the woods which drops down to it. You're Scottish?'

'So are you.'

In the way of womankind worldwide, the two women appraised each other and decided that they liked what they saw, all in the blink of an eye.

'I'll show you,' Jo offered. 'It's near my usual dogwalk.'

'Nice dog,' said Meg, reaching down to smooth the broad forehead.

'Yes. Trouble is, he knows it — and plays on it.'

'Don't they all?'

'I'm Jo. Short for Josephine.'

'And I'm Meg. Short for Megan.'

As easily as that, the two women dropped into walking side by side, past the terraced houses, then through a gateway on to a woodland track.

'I need this exercise,' said Meg. 'I bought enough for two to eat at the market. Then, before I knew it, there was nothing left.'

'You've been at Pickering?'

'Yes. I blame the woman who made that scone . . . it was divine.'

Jo's lips quirked. 'Was it the stall up at the top of the street?'

'Yes,' said Meg, surprised. 'Do you know it?'

Jo nodded. 'I've bought cakes from him as well.' Not strictly true.

'The cakes looked lovely.'

'They're OK,' Jo conceded.

'Looked better than OK to me. How long have you lived here?'

'About seven years. Ever since . . . '

Meg waited. 'Since what?'

'Nothing,' said Jo. 'It's a nice place. Nice people.'

Meg sensed deep hurt. Too deep to probe.

'It's lovely and quiet,' she said. 'In this little valley, you'd never guess there was a busy road only half a mile away.'

'That's the road to Scarborough. It's always busy. Especially in the summer, with holiday folk.' Jo sensed that Meg had sensitively changed the topic, and was relieved. 'Are you down here on holiday yourself?'

'Sort of,' Meg said. 'Do you live in the town?'

'No. Up in Fadmoor — a wee village up at

the edge of the moor. I'm a dog-walker. Ben's one of my regulars.'

Jo was setting a pace up the slope of the dale which was leaving Meg struggling. She stopped. 'What's that noise?' she asked.

'It's a woodpecker.'

'And that one'

'A jay.'

Meg listened, entranced. 'These woods are full of birds.'

Jo smiled. 'The dales are the only places where there's shelter. In the winter the wind howls across the moors, and everything huddles down here, to get out of it. That's why there's trees, and that's why the trees are full of birds.'

'But you like it — even in winter?'

'I love the place,' Jo said quietly. 'Why do you want to see the mill? Are you a photographer?'

'Only with my mobile phone.' Meg laughed. 'No . . . I was just curious. I heard about it somewhere.'

That didn't ring quite true — but two people could be sensitive to each other's feelings. 'It's a lovely place,' said Jo. 'Just above the old ford. This path leads up to the moors.'

'It's a fair old climb,' panted Meg.

'Am I walking too fast? Sorry. I live my life on the gallop.'

'It's that scone,' puffed Meg. 'I shouldn't have eaten it.'

Jo's face broke into a wide smile. 'I baked your scone,' she said. 'So it's me you have to blame.'

Meg leaned against a pine tree. 'You have the touch,' she said. 'My dad was a baker. He wouldn't let us buy cakes. He baked everything himself. He tried to teach me — said I had the hands for it. They're always cold.'

'Perfect, for kneading dough,' said Jo with a smile.

'That's what he said.'

'Is he still . . . ?'

'He died years ago — both him and my mum. Less than a year between.'

'I'm sorry,' Jo said quietly.

They climbed a little further, then the path branched. 'That's your path,' Jo pointed. 'It drops through the firs and pines into natural woodland. When you hear the river, you're getting close.'

'Thanks.' Jo stooped to pat Ben. 'How many dogs do you walk?'

'Four. Sometimes six.'

'Have you more to walk after you take Ben home?'

'No. I'll be rushing for the school bus. To take my kids back home.'

'Kids . . . dog-walking . . . baking. You sound like a busy woman.'

'I am.'

'Then thanks for taking the time to put my feet on the right path.'

'Pleasure.' Jo checked her watch and the hands that ruled her life. 'I can come with you for a bit.'

'That would be lovely — but only if you have the time.'

'I'll make time.'

The two women walked easily down the path, emerging from the darker conifers into the brighter green of broad-leaved woodland. The noise of the river became stronger, and then Meg saw it glistening through the trees.

'There's your mill,' said Jo. 'Pretty as a picture. A shame it's falling into ruin — it's a place meant to be lived in, where somebody could share the silence of the woods.'

'You like it here?'

'Reminds me of the place where I used to do my courting.'

Meg smiled. 'That's a nice memory to have.'

'It is. I'm a widow now.'

Meg stared, stricken. Suddenly the baking, dog-walking, everything, made sense: the air of deep hurt, the toughness. 'I'm ever so sorry,' she said quietly.

'Bad things happen. I shouldn't have

bothered you with it.'

Meg reached out, and touched the woman's arm.

'It's all right,' Jo said unsteadily. 'I can handle it.' Her eyes filled up, to make a liar of her. 'I'd better be going.'

'Jo!' Meg called after her.

'What?'

'That old mill is mine. By inheritance, two days ago. And I don't know why I told you that, either.'

Jo studied the younger woman. It was offered as a secret shared, she guessed, not bragging. 'Maybe we're both daft. So you own that lovely old mill. What are you going to do with it?'

'I don't know. I want to step inside it, and then decide.'

'Why?'

'I just feel I owe that . . . to the man who left it to me.'

'Who was he?'

'Somebody called Henry Waterston.'

'Never heard of him,' Jo said. 'Well, I'm running late. Best of luck.'

Meg hesitated. 'Have you time to come into the mill with me?'

'Not really,' said Jo.

She saw Meg's crestfallen look, and did a quick mental calculation.

'All right,' she said. 'But as soon as you're inside, I must go.'

'Thanks,' said Meg.

Despite the fact she had only met Jo half an hour before, it felt as if she had known her all her life. With the mill looming high and square at the far side of the ford in front of her, she felt a little intimidated; by the building itself, by the decision which she soon must make — and, somehow, because she sensed in the silence and the shadows the presence of the stranger who had left it to her. The small hairs prickled on the back of her neck.

Better to go in there with a friend, she thought.

★   ★   ★

'How did horses and carts cross this ford in winter?' Meg asked, picking her way over the stepping-stones above the shallows.

'Not sure they did,' said Jo. 'They probably used the bridle path down the far side of the river — the one that comes out on the Fadmoor road. It's a metalled track, and better for carts.'

The two women stepped carefully across the worn stones and reached the other side.

'That's better,' said Meg, looking up again.

'Oh, no, Ben. Not that!' groaned Jo.

The old Labrador had waded through the shallows, stopped to lap up the water, then decided he was hot enough to sit down in it. The clear brook water flowed round either side of him as he sat, canine bliss on his face.

'He's not supposed to get into water,' sighed Jo. 'He's got rheumatics. I'll have to towel him dry when I get back.'

On this side of the river, the mill buildings seemed immense. Its large weathered water-wheel was draped in moss and ferns — clearly, it was many years since it had last turned. The sluice was overgrown with water plants, and patches of primroses clung to crevices in the rough stone walls. Three storeys of stone building towered over them, grass growing from the walls and weeds overhanging the guttering. Behind boards nailed across the lower windows there seemed to be grey shutters. On the second storey a few panes of glass were broken, showing dirty, faded curtains inside. The sunlight was so strong it dazzled them as they tried to see the windows of the top floor.

'It's a lot bigger than it seemed from the other side,' Meg whispered.

'First time I've stood here, myself,' Shielding her eyes, Jo peered up.

Across the river a wood pigeon crooned.

42

The only other sound was the river running gently past, heading down the green valley towards Kirkbymoorside.

'It's such a beautiful place,' Meg said quietly.

Jo checked her wristwatch. 'How do we get in?' she asked. 'Will we have to pull some of the boards away from a window?'

'In theory, no.' Meg searched through her bag and pulled out a massive old metal key, the lawyer's label still attached. 'All we have to do is find a door.'

'Round here.' Jo led the way back to the sunny side of the mill.

Paint was peeling from cracked wood on the double door, while the door lock was rusted and thick with cobwebs.

'Does your key fit?' asked Jo.

Meg eased the key into the keyhole, pushed it gently through until she felt solid resistance. Muck — or the other side of the lock?

'Go on, turn it,' said Jo. 'I'm running out of time.'

Meg tried, gently. The key barely moved. She forced it. A creak.

'Here, let me,' said Jo.

The older woman gripped the key firmly, and turned with all her might.

'The lock needs oil squirted into it,' said Meg.

'It's moving,' panted Jo. 'We've done it!'

With a groan of moving metal parts, the lock surrendered.

'Well, go on,' said Jo. 'It's your place, so you should be first inside.'

Meg struggled to turn the rusted door-knob. More creaks, then the heavy door swung slowly open and sunlight laid a shaft of gold across the stone-tiled floor.

'Wow!' said Jo.

They stepped inside, standing carefully in the sunlight, as if the shadows belonged to someone else. There was a huge long dust-covered wooden table, a scattering of wooden chairs, rows of cupboards and some wooden shelving. Then, behind the table, two rusted metal doors were set into a solid brick construction, which had a chimney breast above.

'What's that?' asked Meg.

'An old bakery oven.'

'And what are these metal rods, at the end of the room?'

'Probably the driving gear from the millwheel. They would use water power both to turn the millstones and drive the pulley. I saw one working once.'

'That makes you my official expert,' said Meg. 'What's up the steps?'

'Careful,' Jo warned. 'There might be bats. Sometimes bat colonies take over deserted buildings.'

'Bats?' exclaimed Meg, retreating from the bottom step.

'You're safe enough,' Jo reassured. 'Bats fly by radar and they're more scared of you than you are of them. Don't worry about them, they won't get into your hair.'

'Says who?' Meg asked doubtfully.

'Jim. My husband. That's what he was always telling me.'

'What length was his hair?' Meg demanded.

Jo laughed. 'All of two millimetres long — the standard forces haircut.'

'Then it was easy for him to be brave,' said Meg, smiling. 'Not even bats could get entangled in that!'

'Why didn't I think of that reply myself?' Jo's cheerful face clouded over, laughter draining from her eyes. Then she looked up. 'Do you know, Meg, that's the first time I have ever laughed, really laughed and been happy again, at a memory of Jim.'

'I'm sorry,' Meg said contritely.

'Don't be. That laughter felt good.' She checked her watch. 'Sorry, I really must be going.'

'Can't you wait until I climb the stairs — in case there are bats?'

'Only if you run up them quickly.'

'All right, I will,' Meg said bravely. She climbed the broad dusty steps and stopped, her head and shoulders above floor level. 'Oh, my word . . . '

'Bats?'

'No. The loveliest room. This must be where he lived.'

'Let's see.' Jo pushed past. 'Wow! I see what you mean.'

There were two linked rooms: a large square living-space, with rows of empty bookshelves and a stove in the centre of the wall, then a vast kitchen-cum-dining room beyond. The two rooms were brightly lit by windows round three sides, the blaze of sunlight turning the dirty panes of glass to molten gold, and leaving the grubby curtains mercifully in shadow.

'I'm twenty minutes late,' Jo said at last. She flew down the stairs and out towards the sleeping dog and the stepping stones. Behind her, she heard the grate of dry wood sliding slowly open. Meg had somehow forced a window up and was leaning out, waving.

''Bye,' Meg called. 'Thanks for everything, Jo!'

'Pleasure,' said Jo.

'How about meeting me for lunch tomorrow? By way of thanks.'

'Where?'

'The King's Head. Round about one?'

'Thanks.' Jo snatched a glance at her watch

and groaned. 'Come on, Ben,' she called. 'Time to make like a greyhound. Follow me.'

Then she was off, jumping from stone to stone, and running up the slope beyond into the green woodland that screened the path. Ben stood, stretched, then decided to follow his human — but at a saner pace. Until, halfway over the ford, the thought crossed his mind: she might be waiting for him with a biscuit.

He broke into a trot, then a gallop.

★ ★ ★

'No thanks, Alison. I drink more coffee than is good for me.' Robert Matthews glanced up from his busy desk, smiling at his secretary.

She smiled back, liking her boss, but thinking that he looked tired.

Matthews waited until she closed the office door. He looked at the paperwork and shook his head. Somehow, he couldn't get his mind around its dry legal content today. Normally this was a challenge which invigorated him — like a good crossword. He took off his reading glasses and laid them on the papers.

Discipline. As senior partner, he should be setting an example to one and all, working steadily behind his desk. He grimaced. When he joined his father's practice, he'd thought all the senior partners were dry old fogies. Was that how his younger employees saw him now?

He pushed back his seat and walked slowly to the office window, looking down at the busy pavement and the endless traffic. Only two days ago he had watched a young client with night-black hair and strong, confident shoulders stride down that pavement. Watched until she was lost in the crowd.

Then, as now, he had stared across the city — and felt deeply unsettled. In some mindless way he wanted to be out on a moorland track, walking with a small backpack bouncing on his shoulders, watching the sun chase cloud shadows across the land. It was years since he had last done that; he struggled to count how many. It was before he married, and had become too caught up in both love and legalities, to do frivolous things like walking for pleasure.

One of these weekends he must drive out into the country. Look out his walking boots — or, more likely, buy himself new ones — and turn his face to the wind and sun. Forget the cares and worries of the practice for a few hours. What did they say nowadays, put them on a back-burner? Or was that from twenty years ago? Since Nancy had died, he had fallen out of touch with anything modern.

He stared down, restless and unseeing. That young woman had brought the whiff of the north and its moorlands back into his sober office. As once had the man she'd never met, the gruff Yorkshireman who had left her everything he owned. Matthews gently massaged his temples.

What would she do with her inheritance, he wondered?

Cash in her chips and put the money into stocks and shares, using money to make more money? He shook his head; she wasn't that type, he thought on the basis of two short meetings. She hadn't seemed much interested in the money — more in the man who had left it to her. What would she make of his old mill, when she saw it?

The mobile phone was in Matthews's hand, unbidden. He grunted, surprised, then walked over to his desk. Somewhere beneath that paperwork was Megan Waterston's mobile phone number. He keyed it into his phone, then hesitated.

After all, she had asked him to act for her. Therefore it was only reasonable that he should check out her thoughts on the ancient mill. Perhaps she was needing to talk to someone, get an objective view, a second opinion from someone with no axe to grind.

Matthews smiled ruefully, a smile which

took twenty years at least off his face. Was he still young enough to fall for a younger woman's attractions? No fool like an old one? He considered this possibility, coldly and honestly.

It wasn't that. Dimly, he recognized that she was an unwitting catalyst for something else. But what, and for whom, and why? He shook his head: a catalyst doesn't bother to ask questions, it simply gets on with what it does best. Which is to trigger major and irreversible change in everything around it.

He glanced at his desk. Should he go back to being the sober senior partner, an example to any junior member of staff who happened to drop in? Or should he follow an instinct he didn't understand, and make contact with someone he barely knew — but liked enormously?

His traitor thumb made the decision for him. It pressed the dialling key.

★   ★   ★

Meg had been apprehensive of the mill when first she saw it, and was very glad indeed to have had Jo's company. Now, with Jo gone, she waited in vain for any feeling of unease at being left alone in the tall old building. It never came.

She looked across the sunlit water to the trees beyond. Leaning on the weather-beaten sill, head and shoulders out through the open window, she breathed in deeply. The crisp spring air smelled of woodland, river, and the high moors above. Through the window flowed a wonderful sense of peace, and tranquillity.

She savoured it.

Leaving the window open to ventilate the rooms, Meg looked around. So this was where Henry Waterston had once lived. There would have been books on the cobwebbed shelves, kitchen utensils hanging around her, carpets on the floor and comfortable chairs to sit on.

She found herself smiling. In a bizarre way, seeing his home made her dead benefactor less threatening. He must have loved this place.

Meg slowly climbed the stairs to the top storey, to find that the floor space was divided into two sections. She walked across bare floorboards, and opened the door to her right. Lots of rusting drive shafts, cogwheels and chains were visible, disappearing through a square hole in the floor. The driving gear for the mill. In the centre of the room was what looked like a giant box, sloping down to a hole in its centre. Was that the hopper, into which they tipped the bags of grain? She closed the door gently, and walked across the narrow dark hallway to the other door. Turned the handle. The old wooden door creaked as it opened on unused hinges.

Beyond was a bright, square bedroom, with windows on three sides and golden sunlight streaming through. Meg coughed as dust caught her throat. On the southern wall there was an inbuilt wooden window seat. Someone had once sat there, looking over the distant moors and the dense woodland below.

She struggled with the metal catch on a sash window, then managed to force it open. Gripping the two brass loops at the bottom of the window, she lifted with all her might. At first she met resistance, then the window groaned slowly upward.

Fresh air flooded into the room. Meg inhaled deeply. On impulse, she sat side-saddle on the window seat, her arm on the exposed sill, and looked out. There came to her a feeling of someone smiling, someone who had sat here just like that, many years before. Maybe the woman of the house?

That should have spooked her, but instead Meg felt an overwhelming sense of peace and love wrap itself around her, like a warm and comforting blanket folded round a child by its mother. She felt herself snuggle in.

She had no idea how long she sat there in the sunlight, at one with whatever gentle presence shared the room. It felt as if she was daydreaming, drifting in some sort of timeless haze. Contented and fulfilled.

Then her mobile phone rang, breaking the spell.

Meg fumbled, almost dropping her mobile: 'Hello?' she said breathlessly.

'Miss Waterston? Robert Matthews here.'

She smiled. 'Let's settle on Meg.'

'Where are you? You sound out of breath? Are you walking?'

She sensed a smile behind the words.

'No. I'm sitting in the top floor of my inheritance,' she said. 'Queen of all I survey — woodlands, moorland, a river sparkling in the sun. Take your pick.'

'Can I have all of them?' he asked.

'You're in luck, I'm doing a Manager's Special deal on them today.'

'Then I will send you a blank cheque.' Matthews smiled. 'Package the lot, and send it down to London.' He paused. 'Well, if you're in the Valley Mill, what do you make of it — or is it still too early to know?'

'I wish you were here, Robert,' she said quietly. 'I have never been in such a magical place, not in all my life.'

'What's its state of repair?'

'It looks neglected from the outside. Inside, everything seems sound. But very dusty — the dust motes drifting in the sunlight look like the Milky Way.'

'Better hold a handkerchief to your nose.'

'It isn't that bad. It's only what I've stirred, as I walked through.'

There was a pause. 'So what's your initial reaction?' Matthews asked. 'Do you think it's sound enough to sell on for redevelopment?'

Meg looked around. The walls seemed solid enough to hold back an invading army. 'I think so,' she said.

'Is there easy access to the town — Kirkby-moorside?'

'There's a footpath and stepping-stones across a ford on one side. And on the other, although I haven't been down it, there's a more solid bridle path. From what I can see, that looks like a sturdy old farm road.'

'Excellent,' said Matthews. 'Shall I arrange to get a surveyor up, to value it? Or would you like a few more days to think things over?'

'No need,' said Meg. 'I know exactly what I want to do.'

'Good.'

'I'm not selling,' Meg said quietly.

'Pardon?' Matthews didn't understand why, but his heart lifted.

'I'm staying. I want to see if it's possible to make this old place habitable again.'

Matthews paused. 'Are you absolutely sure? If it has a conservation order, there will be all sort of problems. And you'll need a surveyor, to make sure you're not wasting your time.' He thought quickly. 'Look, why don't I take a few days off, and come up tomorrow morning? Easier to talk things through and sort them out if we are face to face. Where are you staying?'

'The King's Head, in Kirkby.'

'Kirkby?'

'Kirkbymoorside.'

'I'll catch an early train,' Matthews said. 'And bring my walking boots.'

'You'll need them,' Meg smiled.

'Good. Can I ask — exactly why have you decided to keep the mill?'

'That's just it,' said Meg. 'I don't know.'

3

'Over here, Robert!'

Matthews glimpsed Meg waving from behind the ticket barrier. Already she seemed a different woman, he thought; there was a new confidence, a new zest for life. He waved back, waiting patiently in the queue of London travellers.

What it was to be young again, he thought wryly, and to face the new adventure of inheriting an ancient mill from a relative she had never known, and whose death she could scarcely be expected to mourn.

'A good trip?' she asked.

'I planned to read a book,' Matthews answered with a smile. 'Then I glanced up to see sunshine and green fields flowing past the window. I've been glued to the scenery ever since, like a schoolboy dodging school.'

He looked years younger, Meg thought. 'I'm glad,' she said. 'You're travelling light — I was expecting more than a small backpack.'

'I always travelled light,' he smiled. 'Old habits die hard. But I will have to buy myself a new pair of walking boots — my old ones

56

fell apart, when I brushed the dust from them. Have we time to look for another pair in York? Or even walk the Roman walls? I used to do that, every time I visited.'

'We must be back in Kirkby for lunch,' Meg said doubtfully.

'Not a problem,' Matthews said easily. 'I'm here on business — and I mustn't let myself get carried away. Where's your car? Is this it?'

Meg opened her rented car's boot. 'I almost used the Park and Ride — then I thought we would be struggling back with cases. You've not even brought a brief case! I thought lawyers never travelled without at least one of those.'

Matthews dumped his backpack in the Fiesta's boot. 'It's back in London,' he said. 'Keeping my shelves of books company.'

'Best place for it.' Meg edged carefully out of the car park, into the busy street. Then she joined the stop-start queue of traffic into the town centre. 'I can't believe how busy York is, even out of the tourist season,' she muttered.

'The Minster attracts visitors from all over the world,' said Matthews. 'No wonder, it is such a beautiful building. There it is, up ahead. One section of the city wall runs behind it, through the clergy's gardens. Have you ever seen those?'

'No.' Meg braked hard as a cyclist shot out

in front of her. 'Were the walls to keep out cyclists?' she asked breathlessly.

'Cyclists are the new invaders.' Matthews smiled. 'The Romans built the original walls and defensive towers around two hundred AD but, not surprisingly, these fell into bad repair. I think it was the Danes who rebuilt most of these walls in about eight hundred AD — yet they're still called Roman walls.'

'Who were the Romans defending the city against? Was it my lot?'

'The Scots? Unlikely. The Romans would be struggling against half a dozen local tribes in those days. They saw themselves as cultured civilization, and everybody else as barbarians.'

'So that's where you English get it from,' quipped Meg.

The traffic started to move more quickly as they escaped the inner city and its 'bars' or tower gates. In the flat countryside, there was fresh green everywhere. Even the air seemed polished, crisp.

'How long will we be?' Matthews asked, starting to feel hungry after his early start from London.

'About an hour,' said Meg. 'There's no direct route — I was thinking of cutting cross-country from Malton.' She glanced across. 'There's a street market there today. It might have walking boots — just make sure that Princess Anne hasn't tried them on in Halifax . . . '

'Pardon?'

Meg laughed. 'The stallholder told me that, about a pair of shoes he was trying to sell me in Pickering. The market moves around — a different town, each day of the week. I'd imagine that most of its stalls are the same.'

'Lead on.' Matthews leaned back in his cramped seat. 'I don't suppose your market sells sandwiches. I'd a very early breakfast, and — '

'Say no more,' said Meg. 'I will take you to a stall where the scones and cakes are out of this world. Then I'll take you to lunch, where you can meet the wild Scotswoman who baked them.'

'At this rate they'll never see me again in my office.' Matthews sighed.

* * *

Jo walked past the busy bar and pushed uncertainly through the doors of the King's Head restaurant. Over in a quiet corner of the room she saw Meg, sitting across from a tall and dignified-looking man. Both had glasses of wine in front of them and were laughing, looking the best of friends.

Jo's uncertainty increased. Who was this

59

man, and had Meg forgotten about the hastily shouted arrangement up at the old mill, yesterday? Was she barging into some new acquaintanceship and likely to cause embarrassment?

She was on the point of withdrawing when Meg looked up.

'Come in, Jo!' she called. 'Here's two hungry people waiting for you.'

As Jo walked among the tables she saw the man rise politely to his feet and move a chair for her. Unaccustomed to being looked after, she felt flustered, but forced herself to sit down calmly and nod her thanks.

'Robert, this is Jo — the genius who baked that cake for you.'

The man's grey eyes twinkled. 'If that's so, you cannot come more highly recommended,' he said with a smile.

Jo felt herself blush. Ridiculous. 'It probably wasn't my cake.'

It was,' said Meg. 'And, to complete the introductions: Jo, this is Robert — a terrifying London lawyer, until you get to know him.'

'It's a long time since I terrified anybody,' Robert said wryly.

'You don't look much like a lawyer,' Jo commented.

'My jeans and open-necked shirt? I'm dressed for a mixture of business and holiday.

It's the first time for years that I've escaped from my office.'

'Can we eat?' demanded Meg. 'I'm famished.'

They ordered, and the food came through. Jo watched, in quiet admiration, as Robert effortlessly guided the conversation, bringing her seamlessly in as if she had always been there. A real charmer, she thought, but naturally so, not contrived. She found herself relaxed and talking about the mill.

'If you're looking for someone to give you an honest answer about whether it's worth saving,' Jo said, 'then I know just the man. Andy Morris from Rosedale was a top civil engineer who came home to take over his dad's old stone-masonry business. He does all sorts of building work but nobody knows better than Andy what's wrong with an old building, or how to cure it. All the locals use him.'

Meg glanced over at Matthews. 'What do you think?'

'He sounds exactly like what we're needing,' said Matthews.

'Why pay surveyors and architects, only to find that they turn to Andy as well,' Jo argued. 'They're always dragging him out to look at old places — then charging the earth for what they claim was their own assessment.'

Matthews slowly revolved his empty glass. 'When my wife and I used to tour Italy, she made sure to pick the restaurant that the locals used. Not the one recommended by our guide books. And we never once had a duff meal. Locals know best — that could apply to your builder too. Do you have his phone number?'

'No — but I can find it in any directory.'

'That's good enough,' said Matthews. 'More wine?'

'I mustn't — I'm out of the habit of drinking,' said Jo. But she was enjoying herself, and the sense of having company. She wished she could stretch out this meal for a little longer.

'Half a glass?'

'Oh, go on,' she said. 'I'll only be drunk in charge of a dog.'

'You can't do that to Ben,' Meg protested, holding out her own glass.

'Why not? He can lead me there and back. They use Labradors as guide dogs, don't they?'

'Is Ben your dog?' asked Matthews.

'Not really. He's one of the dogs I walk.'

'Are there decent walks around here? The moorlands aren't too far away.'

'No need to climb up there. We've all sorts of walks up the dale. Are you a walker, then?'

'Once, about a hundred years ago.'

'He's bought a new pair of trainers at the market,' said Meg.

'They didn't have boots,' Matthews said by way of excuse. 'I couldn't wait to buy some boots in York, because I wanted very badly to do some walking, while I was here and enjoy some fresh air and exercise.'

'Then stick your trainers on your feet and come with me today,' said Jo. 'But it's only an hour's walk — nothing major.'

'It's years since my last real walk. That sounds ideal.' Matthews looked at Meg, relaxed and sipping the last of her wine. 'Well, are you going to show me that mill of yours?'

'Once we've phoned Jo's builder. You two go ahead — let me bodyswerve this one. All I need you for is to be with me when I meet the builder. How about if I set that for three p.m.?'

'That's fine by me.' Matthews waved the waiter over. 'The bill, please.'

'Not at all,' said Meg. 'This was my treat.'

'Nonsense,' said Matthews firmly. 'I have had the best morning I've known in years. The very least I can do, is collect the tab.'

Meg raised an eyebrow. 'Why not?' she teased. 'You can always add it to my bill.'

'Damn!' said Matthews. 'Rumbled again.'

'Where did you walk before?' asked Jo.

They had climbed up from the mill on to the path through the trees, then walked easily on through the woods, reaching the edge of the local golf course before striking off through fields.

Matthews paused, looking around and savouring the moment.

'Walked?' he eventually replied. 'All over. The Derby peaks . . . the Lakes . . . the Moors, up north near Whitby . . . the Cleveland Way . . . oh, and the Welsh hills.'

'Did you ever walk in Scotland?'

'Yes — I climbed some Munros, before bagging them became a fashion.'

'How about the Borders?'

'Not really. I did some walking around Moffat and St Mary's Loch — but more as evening strolls when I was driving north or south.'

'I came from the Borders,' Jo said. 'Over towards Jedburgh.'

'It has a beautiful old abbey, as I remember.'

'Yes — but with a very dodgy history.'

Matthews fell behind on a narrowing path, then moved alongside again once he had passed the obstacle. 'What brought you down here?' he asked.

'My marriage. More correctly, when my husband was killed.'

'You too?' he said quietly.

'Your wife?'

'Many years ago — a plane crash, in America. I lost both wife and daughter.'

'I'm sorry.'

'She was an American — going home to see her mom. They got caught in one of their extreme weather 'twister' storms. The wreckage showed that the plane had been battered by ice balls, some as big as your fist.'

'Jim was killed in Afghanistan,' Jo said sombrely. 'And that's the second time in two days, when I have talked about it to a stranger.'

'Not a stranger,' Matthews said quietly. 'A fellow casualty.'

They walked on slowly, the old dog forgotten, tiring, and lagging behind.

'Tell me . . . do you ever get over things, so that you don't miss them quite as much?' Jo asked.

Matthews shook his head. 'You learn to live with it — like you would learn to live with an arm or a leg torn away. You cope — maybe even laugh again. But the wound, the feeling of total loss, is always there.'

'For years I used to hear him moving around the house.'

Matthews smiled. 'When I'm untidy, I still hear her scold me — and find myself gathering things up, as she would have wanted.'

Jo laughed. 'Jim was precise and tidy, army style,' she said. 'I was the one who got nagged. Now it's me who chases the kids.'

'How many?'

'Two. Girl of sixteen, bright enough for college — but with the increase in course fees and money tight, I doubt she'll make it. And a lad of fourteen, whose only ambition is to follow his dad into the army. That terrifies me. I don't want to give another hostage up to Britain trying to sort out somebody else's war.'

'Amen,' said Matthews. 'Oh my word . . . look at that view!'

They paused on the last brow of the fields, looking across a small village to the moorland, rising above. A huge blue sky arched over everything, s mall white clouds scampering across it, driven by the brisk Yorkshire wind.

'I don't want to go back to London,' Matthews groaned.

'It's lovely, isn't it? That's Rosedale, over to the right. Away up to the left, that's Bilsdale. They both cut right through the moors.'

'I want to walk them,' Matthews said.

'Oh no!' Jo glanced at her watch. 'I'm an

hour late. I've walked miles further than I meant to. Look at Ben. He's shattered — and I've got to get him back, then pick up my kids.' She looked across at Matthews. 'Sorry, we have to turn back, and we're going to have to run. I don't know if poor old Ben has a gallop left in him.'

Matthews thought quickly. 'Look, you go ahead and collect your kids. I'll walk the dog back at a sensible pace. You can double back and meet us, down at the foot of the path. Would that work?'

'You don't mind being left with Ben?'

'We two old guys will bumble home together.'

Jo hesitated. 'Thanks,' she said. 'In this day and age, you don't want to leave your kids hanging about.'

'Then run!' urged Matthews. 'We'll bring up the rear.'

He watched her flying figure. Nice woman, he thought. Brave — but still vulnerable, given purpose only by having to look after her kids. Easy to be with, easy to talk to. It helped that they had a major loss in common.

Then he stopped in his tracks. He'd forgotten the meeting with the stonemason! When he had promised faithfully that he'd be back in time to help.

Matthews shrugged. Unless he was very much mistaken, Megan Waterston was more

67

than capable of handling that on her own. He turned and gave one last longing look at the moorland. Yes — but on another day.

When he glanced down, Ben was lying flat out, panting, his tongue lolling wearily, soulful eyes watching him. Clearly past his first — and second — bloom of youth.

'You and me both, boy,' he said. 'Come on.'

* * *

Meg was perched in her most favourite window seat in the world, looking out over the dark woods to the rolling Howardian hills beyond the town. The keen spring air brushed past her, like a living thing. She waited for that wonderful sense of peace and belonging to fold itself round her, but it never came.

Instead, she felt a strange sense of anticipation — probably she was on edge over her meeting with the masonry expert. So much depended on his judgement. She heard distant rooks calling, disturbed, then became conscious of a diesel engine growling, coming closer in low gear. Meg straightened. Was this her expert?

Out of the shadows slid the long shape of a Toyota pick-up truck, coming to a quiet stand-still on the sunlit grass in front of the mill. Meg rose, and hurried downstairs, to find a man in his mid thirties, standing with his hands in his pockets and his head tilted back, studying the stone wall towering above him.

'How do,' he said. 'Saw you up at thon window.'

'Megan Waterston,' she introduced herself. 'How do you do, Mr Morris?'

'Right champion. This is your mill?'

'As of a few days ago.'

'And you want an opinion. Are you selling on?'

'I'd rather try to rescue the place, and stay.'

'Waterston, you said? You'll be related to old Henry Waterston?'

'Did you know him?' Meg asked eagerly.

'Nay. But my dad did. Said he was a hard beggar, but a fair one — and he could hold his ale . . . ' Sparkling blue eyes turned to her. 'That's about as good as it gets, for a character reference in Yorkshire.'

Meg laughed. 'He was some sort of distant uncle. I had never met him, I didn't even know he was in my family — but I like that reference.'

'You're Scottish,' he said. 'It's not like a Scotswoman, to throw money at an owld building?'

She felt that he was teasing her — but, in a strange way, testing her too. A local, sussing out a potential newcomer.

'Mebbes aye, and mebbes naw.' She exaggerated her accent.

'So it's depending on what I say? And me, a canny Yorkshireman — the only nation meaner than the Scots.'

'I didn't know Yorkshire was a nation?'

'Oh it is. We don't have much time for the soft South. Or the Midlands. Or the Welsh — and least of all the funny fowk from Lancashire.' Again the blue eyes sparkled. This was clearly someone with an impish sense of fun.

'What do you think about the building, then? Is it rescuable?'

Morris studied the stonework again, taking his time. 'As my owld da would have said . . . eee, lass, but it will be theer when thee an' me are faded photographs on t' piano. Not that we ever had a piano, mind you.'

'So, it can be rebuilt?'

'Might just need howking out weeds and repointing the outside walls, new mastic and putty on the window frames, checking roof timbers and slates. If the walls are as solid as they look, it might only need work done inside, to bring it up to what you want . . . which is?'

'As near the original, as possible.'

'That's good,' said Morris. 'It's liable to have a conservation order on it, to be

70

protected, and it'd likely be the devil's own job to get permission to change. But it's too soon to judge, from here. I'll need to have a prod at it, then look inside. Then climb into the roof space, to check what's there.'

'Feel free,' she said. 'Take your time. I'm expecting someone who will want to speak to you . . . '

'Your husband?'

'My lawyer. He's come up from London, to help.'

'From London? Happen I should have polished me boots.'

'He's not that kind of lawyer,' said Meg with a laugh.

'What kind of lawyer is he, then?' Morris edged round her, hauling out a long, multi-stage ladder from his truck.

'He's a friend, a decent guy. Can I help you?'

Morris grunted. 'If you want — just steady the end o' this. Leave me to carry the weight. Let's set it against t' outside wall.'

'I thought you said inside the roof?'

'Later. I want to see these weeds. I'm not a surveyor, looking at the walls through binoculars. We masons like to get our fingers into the cracks . . . feel how wide and deep they are. Here will do.'

Morris balanced the ladder, hauled out the

top section and locked this into place. Then the mid section. 'It will take scaffolding, to work on 't proper,' he said conversationally. 'But I just want a closer look.'

The ladder creaked as he ascended. He leaned slightly over, tugged out a bunch of weeds. Meg's face was showered in grit. 'Mmm,' he said, and the ladder creaked again as he climbed higher to another bunch of weeds.

This time she stood clear.

'Quick learner,' she heard him say, as if talking to himself.

This time Morris poked and prodded and had a good tug at the ancient mortar which should have been joining and sealing the stones.

'Mmm,' he said again. 'Let's see t' other side.'

The ladder creaked as he came down. She helped him carry it round out of the sun, into the deep shade of the side nearest the river.

'Moss,' he said. 'To be expected. Shade, an' water. Some willowherb, seeded up there. Best have a look. Don't like that sapling that's rooted, up on top floor. Roots can fairly heave the old stones about.'

He grunted as he set the ladder against the wall. Standing well back and shielding her eyes, Meg watched him climb steadily to a tiny twisted sapling, growing almost sideways from the stone wall of the mill. He tugged at it. Nothing happened. 'Mmmm,' he said.

Morris descended and collapsed the ladder into a single length again. 'Let's see your inside rooms,' he said. 'Then up in t' roof space.'

'What do you think, so far?'

'I think I should see the inside rooms, then the roof space,' he said solemnly, but his eyes were twinkling.

'All right.' She gave a sigh. 'I can take a hint. I'll get out of your hair. Here's my lawyer, anyway.'

Meg walked down to the stepping-stones as Matthews came carefully across. 'I'd hate to do this in a spate,' he said. 'Sorry I'm late — we walked further than Jo planned. Then she had to run to catch the school bus. I brought up the rear with Ben. That dog won't need to be rocked to sleep tonight.'

She held out her hand, and he took it naturally, steadying himself for the last long step on to land. 'So our builder has come,' he said. 'What do you make of him?'

'Should that not be 'what does he make of the property?''

'Not really,' said Matthews. 'I want to know if we can trust him, before we hear what he has to say. Builders will tell you to do more than is needed, because the more compli-cated they can make the work, the higher are their profits.'

'He seems pretty straight. Very Yorkshire — more in attitude than accent — and he won't be rushed. He wants to give the place a good looking-over before he commits himself.'

'That's promising.' Matthews fought down a yawn. 'Sorry . . . an early start, followed by a full day in fresh air . . . '

'There's more than Ben will sleep soundly tonight?' suggested Meg.

'Absolutely. Let's go up and see what your builder has to say.'

'No. Let him take his own time. I think he knows his stuff, so let's give him space to look over the mill.'

'Agreed,' said Matthews. He sat heavily on a rock. 'I should have broken these trainers in more gently. Myself as well. Gone are the days when twenty miles was a stroll. And even better, if I threw in a hill or two to climb along the way.'

Meg perched on the far side of the rock, and together they watched the river wimpling past through the stepping-stones.

'It's a beautiful valley,' he said. 'And this is an idyllic spot.'

'That makes two of us who think that way.'

'Three at least,' said Matthews. 'There was old Henry too, and his folks . . . then probably another generation at least before them.'

'Old Henry was a hard beggar — but he could hold his ale.'

'Who says?' Matthews looked up, amused.

'Andy Morris's dad.'

'It's a recommendation of sorts.'

'As good as it gets, he assured me.'

Matthews laughed. 'North countrymen don't try too hard with their compliments,' he said, heaving himself to his feet. 'Here's your builder, let's hear what he has to say.'

They walked to meet Morris, who had dropped his ladder on to the grass, and was studying the building with his hands on his hips. He turned, as they approached. 'Your London lawyer?' he asked.

'None other. Robert Matthews.'

'Andy Morris.'

The two men shook hands, the mason's skin calloused and dry to the lawyer's soft hands. 'Well,' Matthews asked. 'What's your opinion?'

Morris looked back at the mill. 'Happen she's sound,' he said quietly. 'I'm pretty sure there's nothing structurally wrong with her. I've still to go round the old millwheel — with the damp and weeds there could be problems there, but the rest is dry. Internal walls are sound, no sign of damp at their base. No sign of rot or recent infestation in the timbers — nor in the roof space either.'

'That's good. So it can be made habitable?' Matthew asked.

'Anything can, if you throw enough money at it. But my guess is that there's only cosmetic work needed — if the lady wants to restore it to how it was. More work, if she wants to redesign the room spaces. For that, we'd have to check its status — could be a conservation order. I'd be surprised if there wasn't, it's a cracking example of an old Yorkshire mill.'

'Would I be crazy to think of living here?' Meg asked quietly.

'Why shouldn't you? If you don't mind being at the end of a track.'

'Would it take long to make enough of it habitable — so that you could work round about me to finish it off?'

'Depends on how you define habitable.'

'Able to be lived in. Running water. Electricity. No frills.'

'I'd need to check pipes and cabling. If they're usable, we're talking of a couple of weeks. If we need to replace them, make that a couple of months. But I could be working on the mill while we waited.'

Meg took a deep breath: 'How much will this cost?'

Morris's eyes flicked to Matthews. 'You have a choice,' he said quietly. 'I can send you

76

an estimate which is high enough to cover any problems that I haven't seen. The daft beggar estimate, it's called in the trade. If you're daft enough to accept, then we know we shouldn't finish out of pocket and, if we're lucky, we could make a bundle.'

'Or?' asked Matthews, level-eyed.

The stonemason met that stare.

'Or you trust me with the job,' he said calmly. 'Give me two full days to crawl over and under her and I'll tell you what I can do over the first two weeks, and where I think we might hit problems. And I'll cost that out. Then when we get that lot finished, I tell you what's next, and we agree a price on that.'

'What happens if your bill runs out of control?' Matthews asked.

'It won't. Give me a ballpark figure of what you want to spend, and I'll work inside that and give you the chance to opt out at any stage of the work. At the end of the day, my costs and wages are covered, and you won't have to pay the safety margin I build into my estimate, to cover my back.'

'You've stopped talking like a Yorkshireman,' said Meg.

'Right. You're talking to the civil engineer.'

Matthews turned away to stare at the river for a few minutes.

Morris waited patiently.

'It's a big ask, in this day and age,' Matthews said slowly. 'If you came to me in London with a proposition like that, I'd tell you to let me think on it. Then I'd contact somebody else.'

'This isn't London. I'm offering you the cheapest way to sort out the mill.'

'With a written contract to that effect?'

'On a handshake. That's how we work up here. In t' North.'

The last words were spoken quietly but with an exaggerated accent.

Matthews smiled. 'Why am I tempted to trust you?' he asked.

'It's the baby-blue eyes.' Morris turned to Meg. 'It's your mill, so it's your shout, lass,' he said.

'He's my adviser.'

'And I'm your stonemason. He knows his stuff. I know mine.'

'It's a deal,' said Meg.

She held out her hand, expecting to have it crushed. She found it gently squeezed and released.

'I spared you the spitting bit,' Morris said amiably. 'Up here, we generally spit into our hands, before we shake and seal the bargain. My da will be spinning like a top in his grave because I didn't do it proper.'

'We can't have that,' said Matthews. He

hesitated, then spat into his hand, and held it out. He got a firm — if slightly sticky — handshake in return.

'You're right, lass,' said Morris, wiping his palm on the seat of his dusty work jeans. 'He's a decent lad — for a lawyer.'

* * *

Robert Matthews lay listening to the distant noise from the hotel bar. His sheets smelled clean and the bed was surprisingly comfortable. Or maybe he was so tired that even a bed of nails would suffice tonight. He couldn't believe the amount of trust he'd given Morris — yet it was surprise he felt, not worry. The Yorkshireman wouldn't let them down.

In the darkness his mind settled slowly into sleep. Fleeting images of himself striding across that moorland, the sun on his shoulders. Then the patchwork quilt of sunshine and shadows in the wood.

The last image, coming just as he slipped over, was of the figure of a woman running lithely down the slope in front of him, her hair streaming out. He wondered briefly who it was — too tall for Nancy.

She turned to laugh back at him and, as he tried to see her face, he fell deeply and contentedly asleep.

Further along the corridor Meg snuggled down, wrapping the hotel duvet round herself. It was still early enough in the spring for the nights to have a bite of coldness in them.

Soon, it would be her own bed she was lying in, listening to the sound of the wind and the river passing by. That window seat would be hers, whenever she chose to use it. She was too tired to be excited. But she knew, at some deep level in her soul, that she had found the place where she was meant to be. If only Henry Waterston was still alive, she could have told him.

Because he too had listened to the water flowing round the stepping-stones.

Her mind slipped sideways; she trusted Andy Morris. Hewn from a similar gruff block of sandstone as old Henry Waterston, but saved from being dour by the laughter that was never far from his eyes. Instinctively she felt that these Yorkshiremen both called things as they saw them. Then took pride in proving themselves to be men of their word.

A rare species, these days. An unknown man had given her the chance to reinvent herself and change her life. Another unknown man had stepped into her life, with the crucial skills to make that happen.

One day, she must find out more about
Henry Waterston. Maybe knowledge of the
man would crack the code of that strange
message he'd left behind.

*Close the circle, lassie, and make it
right . . .*

She drifted off.

4

In the early morning stillness the river and its trees looked like a painting. Only the murmur of water squeezing through between the stepping-stones threatened to break the illusion. Meg sat on her window seat, the window open in front of her, looking out over the green of the tree tops to the distant hills.

'I can see why you like it up here,' Matthews murmured. 'There's such a wonderful sense of peace — inside the room, as well as out in the valley.'

'I don't want to live anywhere else,' Meg said simply. She turned round and smiled. 'Are many of your clients as nutty and self-indulgent as me?'

Matthews grinned. 'You'd be surprised.'

'But it all makes work for the working lawyer to do?'

'Exactly.'

They stared out over the valley. Somewhere in the distance, a rook called, looking for company. Only the river answered.

Meg sighed. 'While Andy is starting work I really must go back to Edinburgh and check my flat. I wasn't planning to be away for as long as this; there will be letters, papers, all sorts of stuff piling up there.'

Matthews nodded, his eyes on the distant hills.

'What should I do with it — the flat, Robert?' she asked.

He blinked, visibly switching on his legal mind and struggling to be professional. 'Your flat? Don't do anything rash. It's important that you take your time before making any decision, especially one which could be as life-changing as coming down here to stay. So don't sell-up.'

'Should I rent it out then?'

Matthews pulled a face. 'That's a minefield, with sitting tenants law these days, at least down in England. Plus there's always damage — people don't take as much care of your property as you would yourself.'

'But I'll maybe need the money?' A lifetime of watching every penny had left its mark on Meg.

Matthews smiled. 'Need money? Why? You're a rich woman.'

It was Meg's turn to blink. 'I keep forgetting,' she said ruefully. 'But what if the work on the mill eats up all the money I was left?'

'It won't,' Matthews reassured her. 'As your lawyer, I will be keeping a tight check on that. I will only countenance reconstruction work which is done within a budget that leaves you enough money to live on, indefinitely. It would be crazy to plunge everything into Henry's old mill. He didn't.'

'True. I'm still adjusting . . . everything happened so quickly.'

'That's why you mustn't make a quick decision on your Edinburgh flat.'

'OK. Good advice. So I will only go back for a few weeks, until Andy has rescued enough of the mill to let me live in it. And while I'm up in Edinburgh, I will try to settle all my affairs for a longer break away. And get my car serviced — it's been screaming for proper work to be done on it. But I'll probably drive Andy mad, phoning up every day to see when I can come back.'

Matthews laughed. 'I can imagine,' he said. 'But as your adviser, let me suggest that you leave room in your mind for the opposite to happen. As in having second thoughts. Once you are back in familiar surroundings, you may find that what has happened down here seems like a holiday you've enjoyed. Wonderful, but not sustainable in the long haul. Don't just bat these thoughts away, Meg. Give them time to make their point, and be ready to rethink your plans. It is always possible to sell the mill. So long as Morris has his costs covered, any work also improves the old building for a sale.'

'Never!' Meg was astonished with the vehemence of her own reply.

Matthews held up his hands. 'It's my job to play devil's advocate, and put the alternative case in front of you. Don't shoot me!'

'Sorry,' Meg apologized. 'It's just . . . to sell this old place is unthinkable.'

'OK. But if you have second thoughts . . . '

Meg forced a smile. 'I will do exactly as you say, and give them serious consideration. What are you planning to do yourself, Robert? When are you going back to London? Will we go back to York in the car together?'

Matthews's gaze drifted up to the distant hills.

'Probably not,' he said after a few moments. 'You should never give slaves a holiday — I don't want to go back, any more than you want to sell. I think I'll take a bit of an overdue holiday. Maybe a week or so, to walk those hills out there, and explore the moorlands up to the north. I'll maybe rent a car, to take me to all the walks I'd like to do. There are all sorts of long-distance paths, both inland and coastal. It's a walker's paradise.'

Meg smiled. Somehow, the older lawyer had become a friend — indeed, was threatening to become almost family. It was a nice feeling.

'You deserve the break,' she said encouragingly.

'My thoughts exactly,' he said cheerfully. 'It's high time somebody else worried about the business for a change.' Then he glanced up. 'Here's our man.'

They clattered down the wooden stairs out into the sunshine, to find Morris unloading his pick-up truck. 'So you got here in front of me?' he said. 'Any chance you are here as volunteers? Ready to do my labouring for me? Carry ladders, mix mortar, saw the wood, make my tea . . . '

'Fan it until it reaches the right temperature?' Meg asked.

'Exactly. I can see you've served your builder's apprenticeship.' Morris's eyes were dancing. 'Stir my sugar at least, break open the packs of sandwiches, nip back to the village for a pasty, or a pinch of salt. That sort of stuff.'

'While you do the skilled work,' Matthews added drily.

'Absolutely. Somebody has to.' He glanced up at the old building. 'Well,' he said quietly. 'Let's get started. First job is to sort out exactly what needs to be done, to make the place fit to sleep in. Then agree the initial cost.'

'Whatever it takes,' said Meg.

Morris smiled at Matthews and sighed.

'I'm glad she has a lawyer, watching over her,' he said.

⋆ ⋆ ⋆

Jo paused at the top of the field and glanced at the moors rising slowly but steadily above Fadmoor. On the public right of way, there was a solitary figure heading back towards the village. An early-season tourist, probably. She turned away, whistling to bring back the small terrier she was walking.

Something made her shade her eyes and look back again.

At first she wasn't sure, then she was. It was the London lawyer. Jo turned to finish the walk, then hesitated, her back to the distant figure. He couldn't possibly have seen her, not well enough to recognize her. And she was with a different dog, one he didn't know. But she had seen him.

She found that she couldn't coldly walk away, so she turned back and went slowly up the path to meet him.

'I thought it was you,' he said quietly.

'You're limping,' she said.

'A blister. My ambition was stronger than my feet. It's these new trainers.'

'It's the daftie who is wearing them.'

Matthews grinned. 'It's years since anyone told me the truth,' he said.

'Where have you been?'

'Way up the dale at the head of this path

87

. . . I don't know which one it is, I have still to buy a proper map.'

'It's Bransdale. Did you go up to where the track loops west?'

'That's where I should have turned.'

'But you didn't,' she said with a sigh. 'When God made men he forgot to put in some common sense.'

'With common sense, I wouldn't have climbed into these lovely hills at the head of the dale. What are they?'

'The Cleveland hills — they run all the way down to Sutton Bank.'

'And the Cleveland Way runs through them, and loops over to the coast — I've walked the coastal bit before, but never the inland one.'

They headed slowly back to Fadmoor.

'You can barely walk,' she said accusingly.

'I'm fine. I'll get there — but I'm going to ditch these trainers and buy proper walking boots. I have old-fashioned feet. They weren't designed for modern trainers. I'm thinking of going into York tomorrow, from Malton. I'll hire a car, and shop around there for a proper pair of walking boots. I might even walk the Roman walls again — have you ever been there, Jo?'

'I've read about them — and I've heard about them. But walked them, no.'

Matthews limped on for a few minutes. He wanted desperately to ask the question, but feared with all his heart that it would be misunderstood. Or even cause offence.

'Would you like to come and walk the walls with me?' he blurted out at last.

Jo stopped, then walked slowly on.

'As a friend,' he said quietly. 'As Meg's friend and therefore, I hope, my friend too. It is so much more fun to walk the walls with somebody, and to be able to chat about what you see from them. The city has spilled out beyond them, so the walls take you through back gardens, across busy streets. It's a cross-section of York's history as a city. Once I knew that history, like I knew my own name. I would love to share what I remember of it with someone.'

'That would be nice,' said Jo. 'It really would. But I can't come with you — I just don't have enough free time in my day.'

'No problem,' Matthews said easily. But she sensed that he was disappointed, maybe even hurt.

'It's not you, Robert,' she said simply. 'Although, God knows, it's years since any man asked me to share something with him. I would like to come — as a friend — I really would. But I'm baking from five in the morning, to deliver to the market by half past seven. Then there's the kids to chase out for the school bus. Then four dogs to walk — two of them twice, morning and afternoon. Then my kids to pick up from school, and do all the usual mum's routine of chasing them to get their homework done, feed them, get them to bed at a proper hour. There's no time in the day for myself — that's just the way it is.'

'I didn't realise,' Matthews said. 'I'm sorry.'

'I'm a widow-woman. I have to do all that work to make ends meet.'

'I understand. And I'm sorry to have embarrassed you.'

Jo stopped, and waited until he turned round to face her. Then she met his look, level eyed. 'I'm not embarrassed,' she said quietly. 'You're a nice guy, sensitive, polite, not pushy. You're offering me friendship, and I am happy to accept that, in the same way as it is offered. I like Meg, I like you. I would like to count you both among my friends — I don't have many. It is purely and simply that I'm a working woman, and can't take time off to come and walk the walls with you. As a friend.'

Matthews smiled. 'Understood. Let's leave it there,' he said.

'No.' Jo's impulse surprised her. 'I can't. That foot of yours, the one that's blistered.'

'I'll survive,' Matthews looked rueful. 'It's not the first blister I've had.'

'And I'm a soldier's widow. It's not the first blister I've treated.'

Matthews looked at her uncertainly.

Jo made up her mind and went for it. 'I live down there — just a couple of hundred yards away in the village. Let me look at your blister, and see what I can do to ease it. Then I'll run you back to your hotel in my car. But you'll have to wait in my house until I've got rid of Jackie. He lives at the other end of the village.'

'I can wait outside,' he said, embarrassed.

'You can wait inside, with your foot dressed, and a cup of tea at your elbow.'

Matthews looked more cheerful. 'Are you sure?'

'Would I have offered, if I wasn't sure? There's no one in the house.'

Matthews sighed. 'It's just . . . I'm not used to having people look after me.'

'I'm not looking after you,' Jo said firmly. 'I'm patching up your feet, then sending you packing. Just like you would do for any friend.'

'Yes ma'am,' said Matthews. 'Message understood. And . . . thanks.'

'You won't say that when I've a sterilized needle in my hand.'

'Can you make that cup of tea a brandy?' Matthews pleaded.

* * *

Sitting alone in her Edinburgh flat, Meg screwed up her face. Without the company that she'd enjoyed during the last few days, her coffee tasted sour and flat. Or perhaps that was more a state of mind, than a taste. She pushed the mug away and got up, walking restlessly over to the window.

She was bored and unhappy. And in the wrong place; after years of living here she simply did not want to be in Edinburgh any more. Her flat seemed small, the road outside almost as noisy and busy as London. She wanted silence, broken only by the sound of birdsong, or a river winding down its green valley. She wanted blue skies and small white clouds — not the chill grey wind which was blowing in from the east along the Forth estuary. Spring came so much later up here in the north.

After all the excitement of the last few days she felt drained and stranded in limbo. Nothing up in Edinburgh seemed to have meaning. She had moved on now. The past no longer mattered, and she couldn't wait to get started on her future. Second thoughts on the mill? As if!

At times she feared that she had dreamed it all, and she had rushed to read through the lawyer's letter again, to reassure herself that the inheritance was real. The signature at the bottom of the brief text was that of someone who was now a friend and a man whom she found herself trusting instinctively. She missed both him and Jo.

Meg glanced at her watch. This would be the dog-walking section of Jo's busy day, so there was a fighting chance that she would be out and walking some track, burning off any exuberance in her companion by the pace she set. Meg smiled. She had Jo's mobile phone number — that had been one of the last things she collected before coming north. But did she know her well enough to crash in for a lonely chat?

Probably not — but she scrolled down to the number, pressed the dialling key and waited, staring out of the window as the phone rang.

'Hiya, Jo,' she said. 'It's Meg. Can you talk?'

Jo struggled to swap the leash over into her left hand.

'Hi, Meg,' she said, a little breathlessly. 'Is there a problem?'

'Not really. I'm just wanting to talk. All the stuff that I thought would take weeks to organize, like banks and car servicing and redirecting post, I cleared up in a couple of days. Now I'm at a loose end, killing time and wandering round my flat like a lost soul. How are you getting on?'

'Busy,' said Jo. 'When did Andy say that he'd be ready to let you move in?'

'He didn't. So I've got the fidgets. I don't know whether I will be hanging around up here for days, or weeks, or months.'

'Then phone him up.' Jo hauled back an over-enthusiastic dog, which had bolted across the path and almost tripped her.

'What's it like down there?'

'Windy — can't you hear it rush across the phone?'

'A bit. Is it sunny?'

Jo sighed. 'Is it a weather report you're wanting? Or just somebody to tell you to come down and live in the King's Head until the mill is ready?'

'That's what I want to do. But it's stupid — costs money.'

'You have money.'

'Yes, but I could be needing it for all sorts of things in the mill.'

Jo stumbled over a tree root.

'Are you all right?' Meg asked.

'Not looking where I was going. Phone Andy, he won't bite you.'

'He won't think I'm nagging, will he?'

'You're his client. He's paid to be nagged. But Andy's laid back, he can handle that.

Phone him, then get back to me and we'll sort something out.'

'OK,' said Meg. 'I will.'

She rang off, feeling better for the brusque advice the no-nonsense Scotswoman had given her. Go for it while she was on a roll, she thought. She searched for the builder's number, then pressed the dialling key. The phone rang on and on. She was just about to cancel the call when he answered.

'Andy Morris here.'

'Meg Waterston.'

'Hey, I'm not finished yet,' he said.

'I'm at a loose end up here, and desperate to come back. How long is it going to take before there's enough of the mill ready to be lived in?'

'Whoa — hold your horses!' he said in mock protest. 'Not long. I've got the roof mended, and most of the pointing done on the weather side. Nothing major up with either o' them. There's a bit of glazing will have to be done, where glass has gone or is cracked. If you bunked in the living area, that would speed things up — only one floor to get ready. I could work round you and do the rest later. Your main problem is there's no electricity yet — at least none I would trust. I'll have to get an electrician in to rip out the old wiring and replace the lot, switches,

95

lights, everything. I know someone who will do a decent job for you.'

'Will it take long?' she asked.

'Not in an old house,' Andy replied. 'Most of their wiring is behind wooden skirting boards or door frames — all I need to do there is ease out the panel, and get rid of it. The only damage is where we have to rip out the old stuff from under the plaster to the switches. In fact, it would help us both if you were here to talk about what sort of lighting you want, and where.'

'So how long will all this take?' Meg felt she was chasing him ruthlessly, and winced.

However, as before, he worked through things in an order which made sense to his own mind, and wouldn't be hurried. 'Water's OK. You have your own stream and boulder-filtered reservoir tank up above the mill — gravity feed, a nice neat job, whoever did that. Give me five days to finish glazing, rewiring, plastering, then you can come in — so long as you don't mind using paraffin lamps for a bit. We will need to replace the external cabling up the track from the band's practice hut — that's an electricity board job, but I can call in some favours. Give them a couple of weeks, but you'll be living with nowt but cold water until then. And eating out.'

Meg's heart lifted. 'Doesn't matter. I'll be there,' she said.

'Hang on. You can't live on bare boards.'

'I can bring my stuff down from Edinburgh.'

'In a big removal van? It would never get up t' track.'

'Oh . . . I never thought of that. What will I do then?'

'Bring basics down with you in t' car, cups, saucers, kettle, pots, bedding, towels and stuff like that. There's plenty places where we can buy some nice old furniture and rugs for a song. Make the mill right homely. I can ferry it up t' track in my truck.'

'But that's putting you to a lot of trouble.'

'It will save your phoning me, every two days . . . '

Meg swallowed. 'Andy . . . thanks. But I'll pay for any help . . . '

'No need. See you in four or five days, then?'

'You'll see me tomorrow. I'll stay at the King's Head until the mill is ready.'

'That's good,' he said easily. 'Buy me a pint, and we can call it quits.'

'It's a deal,' said Meg.

★ ★ ★

Robert Matthews leaned on the white limestone, and watched sunlight bathe the ornate stonework of the Minster. He had enjoyed walking the Roman Wall which had been deserted. He'd had it almost to himself — apart from this busiest section, which featured in every guide book. He found himself buffeted from the back, as a guided party pushed past.

It had been a good day. He was tempted to do another lap of the wall and its linking street section, but had learned his lesson yesterday. When wearing new boots, don't ask them or your feet to do too much at once. He wriggled his toes; Jo had made a perfect clinical job of lancing the sore blister, then dressing the wound. A nurse couldn't have done better.

Gradually, the bulk of the Minster slipped out of focus. He saw through it and past it. Jo was a nice woman. Lonely, but guarded, and doing what it took to make ends meet for her family until they were able to fend for themselves. As a lawyer, Matthews routinely met many women, both colleagues and clients. Few, if any, had made such a deep impression.

Dangerous territory? No, just simple friendship. A shared sense of loss, giving an instant understanding of each other's scar tissue and mood swings.

He moved restlessly. At some stage soon he should be thinking of getting back to London. But not yet. For the first time in many years, he was behaving irresponsibly — and enjoying every minute. Tentatively, he stamped the injured foot. Still sound. His cheap trainers had been taken into a charity shop, and their replacement lightweight boots weren't half the trouble . . . worth every penny of costing five times as much.

Idly, he pondered how best to get back to his newly rented car. Complete his circuit of the wall, then walk back through the cobbled streets past the Minster? Descend through the nearest barbican, and retreat to the car park? He pushed himself away from the limestone wall, heading back to the Monks' Bar, stepping aside to let a party of schoolchildren pass. Reaching the tower he descended the narrow and deeply worn steps, then walked through the sharp shadows in the street towards his car.

Part way along the road out of town he passed a sweet shop. He hesitated outside, then went in and bought the biggest box of chocolates he could find. Paid for it, tucked it under his arm, then headed back into the street.

Once there, he frowned. Why had he bought these, almost on automatic pilot? He hated chocolates, never ate them. And the only person to whom he could give them would only be embarrassed by his impulse buy.

However, she had mended his foot and he wanted to say thanks. How did you say thanks to a woman these days? Flowers? Chocolates?

The box seemed to grow bigger by the minute in his hands. Too big to change his mind and stuff into a litter bin.

He grimaced. Never act on impulse was his standard advice to any client. He would leave the chocolates in the car and decide what to do with them later.

★ ★ ★

Meg didn't mean it to happen quite that way. Having parked in the town, she meant to stroll down to the stepping-stones and the mill and surprise Jo and Ben, out on their last walk of the day. It wasn't in the script that she should stumble a little on a tree root, then not just trot a couple of steps to regain her balance, but to keep on trotting down the path. It seemed easier to keep going than to stop. She jogged through the conifers and out into the green cathedral of the broad-leafed natural woodland, the sunlight spilling gold through the fresh colours of spring.

She stopped, panting, when she came out

into the clearing at the riverside. It was still there, the mill: no figment of her imagination, but square and solid as a castle built out of yellow Yorkshire sandstone.

Her mill. And, she knew with every fibre of her being, her future.

Meg felt a wave of relief, as if she had just come home. She walked slowly down to the stepping-stones, to stop and listen to the liquid murmur of the river gliding through them. This was the sound she had craved to hear. On impulse, she reached down and gathered two handfuls of the clear cold water, washing her hands in it, then raising them to spread its healing touch across her eyes and face.

'Haway, lass! Tha'll poison t' fishes.'

Meg shot bolt upright, looking across the sunlit space. It was Andy, leaning out of the mid-floor window, and waving down to her.

'Hello,' she called across; then, self-consciously, she picked her way over the stones towards the mill.

He was waiting for her on the far bank. 'What kept thee?' he demanded. 'I was expecting thee at ten past eight this morning . . . '

'I slept in,' she said sheepishly, conscious of the water running down her face.

'Here,' he said, fishing out a white handkerchief, still in its folds. 'I keep this 'un for visitors.'

'You don't!'

'Nay — but it's a good line.' His blue eyes were dancing, just as she had remembered. 'Where's t' car?'

'Up in the town. Outside the King's Head. I'll be staying there tonight.'

'Have you booked in?'

'No. It was empty last week. Why? Is there a problem?'

'Happen it's the annual convention of the Yorkshire Fettlers and Ferreteers — it will be full to the roof tonight.'

She stared at him, suspicion growing. 'Andy, you're winding me up,' she accused. 'There's no such thing as a fettler or a ferreteer.'

'Oh, we've fettlers,' he said grandly. 'It's the ferreteers that are a bit thin on t' ground. Mun be the lack of pure-bred Yorkshire ferrets.'

'Stop it,' she laughed. 'And stop talking like a Yorkshire yokel.'

He grinned. 'It's the way I talk,' he said broadly. 'It was the language of my childhood. I went to university, talking like that and punched the living daylights out of anybody who laughed. Then I learned to speak proper college English, like the rest of them. I'm bilingual, now. And confused.'

Meg felt happy, as if a huge cloud had lifted and the sun had broken through. 'I had to see my mill again,' she said. 'Couldn't wait.'

'You came haring out of these woods as if the devil was chasing you.'

'Didn't mean to,' she said. 'Have you seen Jo or Robert today?'

'No. Why?'

'I thought they might be here,' she said uncertainly. 'I texted Robert that I was coming down.'

'He might not have read it — might have been in traffic somewhere.'

'That's true,' she said. 'Well, aren't you going to show me what you've done while I've been away up north? Or is it so little that I'll barely see the difference?'

'Eee, lass,' he said. 'What's tha hurry? When t' Good Lord made time, he made plenty of it.'

*   *   *

'Where have you been?' Jo asked.

Matthews started in surprise. 'Sorry. I didn't see you come up.'

'It's a skill I've got. All mothers have it. We creep up and pounce.'

He laughed. 'My mum had it too, now that

you mention it. I've been down in York, hiring this car and going for a walk round the walls.'

'So they're still there then, the walls?'

'As of three p.m.,' he said. 'Give or take a few minutes.'

'Good. I'll rest easier tonight. What are you doing?'

'Checking my mobile phone. I think a text came in, but I was driving. Then I thought it would be the office chasing me, and left it until I'd finished walking the walls. Then I simply forgot. I only remembered as you came creeping up.'

He glanced down at the mobile's screen. 'Drat. It's from Meg — she's coming down again today.' He looked up blankly. 'What's she coming down for? The mill won't be ready for weeks.'

'She's going to stay in the hotel for a few days. Andy says he will have enough of it sorted out for her to move in by the end of the week. When did she send the text?'

'Don't know. Yes, I do. Mid morning. I had better text her back.'

'No need,' said Jo. 'Go and surprise her instead.'

'Where will she be? The hotel?'

'Think again — the mill.'

'Of course. I'll nip down to see her now — are you coming?'

Jo shook her head. 'Just waiting for the school bus to come in, and collect my kids. Are these new boots? Are your feet fit to do another walk in them?'

Matthews grinned. 'See,' he said, stamping his foot. 'I'd me the best nurse in the world . . . oh . . . ' He turned round to look into the boot of the hired car.

She followed his eyes, to the large box of chocolates. Just thrown in anyhow. 'Oh,' she said. 'What are these? Have you a sweet tooth?'

Matthews flushed crimson. Then he shrugged.

'I bought them for you,' he mumbled. 'By way of saying thanks. Then decided that you might take offence — feel it was too familiar. When it was only meant as the gesture of a friend and grateful patient.'

'So long as that's all it was,' she said.

'Why, yes — of course.'

Her wary eyes softened. Jo liked this shy and sensitive man.

'Well,' she said. 'I'm waiting for it. This gesture from a friend and patient.'

'Oh . . . I should have wrapped them up.'

'And wasted an Amazonian forest in packaging?'

Robert handed them over. 'By way of thanks,' he said. 'Enjoy them.'

'I will,' she said quietly. 'And Robert?'

He turned back warily, poised for flight. 'Yes, Jo?'

'Thanks, I love chocolates, and it's years since I could afford to buy any.'

'Do you know what?' he said, relieved.

'What?'

'I wish the shop had stocked an even bigger box.'

5

The knock on the kitchen door was quiet, but persistent. Impatiently, Jo scrubbed a floury hand over her face. Nobody else could hear it, therefore nobody else would answer it. Other than herself.

'Turn down that television!' she shouted, wiping her hands on a towel. Drat! More mess she would have to clear up. In a thoroughly grumpy mood she opened the back door. 'Oh, it's you,' she said, surprised.

'Guilty,' said Meg. 'Have I come at a bad time?'

'If it's between six a.m. and ten p.m. it's bad,' Jo grimaced. 'Come in — what are you doing here anyway?'

'Killing time,' said Meg.

Jo stared at her silently.

'Wrong words,' Meg apologized. 'What I meant was that I'm too restless to settle, and you're the only friend I've got down here. I guessed you would be baking for tomorrow morning. Can I help?'

This was the first time for years that anybody had offered help, and Jo found herself fighting back tears. 'Can you bake?' she asked.

'My dad said I could — and he was a baker.'

'I've measured out flour for three dozen scones, that's the most I can get into my oven. Can you mix it for me?'

'I can try. Where do I wash my hands?'

'Lift out these used trays. I'll be washing up later. Here's the sultanas . . . '

'I know. Mix them in while the flour is dry. It spreads them better through the dough.'

'That's right. I'll start measuring out the cake mixes.' Jo watched out of the corner of her eye, then relaxed. 'Your dad was right, you have the hands for it,' she complimented.

Meg worked away. 'All that stuff you bake, is it for the same market stall?'

'Yes. He wants me to do more, but I'm already battering my oven into the ground. I need a proper industrial oven.'

'How much are those?'

'A fortune. I've neither the space nor the money. So we stays as we are, a cottage industry.'

'Real home-baking . . . will I use this to cut out the scones?' Meg asked, having gently rolled the dough on a baking-board dusted with flour.

'That's it.' Jo frowned in concentration as she organized the ingredients for her cake — the first of several. 'Have you seen that

108

Robert today?' she asked.

'Yes. We'd dinner together. Why?'

'No reason. Just . . . I bumped into him earlier, when he came back from York.' Jo blushed at the thought of that huge box of chocolates, and hoped that Meg would put the heightened colour down to the heat which was building up to sauna level in the small kitchen. The downside of her cottage industry.

Meg was too busy cutting out scones to notice. 'It's weird,' she said. 'A couple of weeks ago I didn't know he existed. Now he's a real friend, who happens to be a lawyer — rather than a lawyer who is easy to work with.'

'Know what you mean,' said Jo. 'Scoot! We're busy here . . . ' this last was directed at a young teenage boy who had stuck his head round the kitchen door.

'But I'm hungry, Mum,' he complained.

'Then you should have eaten more at dinner.'

'I hate stew. Is there a packet of biscuits?'

'Third cupboard on the right, top shelf. Remember, these have to last till the end of the week. Meg, this is Jamie, whose stomach has no memory . . . '

'Hiya,' said Meg, looking up from the tray of scones.

'Hi,' he said shyly. He grabbed the biscuits and disappeared.

Jo groaned. 'I have one I can't fill, and another I can't get to eat — in case it makes her fat. It's a constant battle, watching them both.'

She glanced over. 'Good, that was quick work. Just slide the trays into the oven — take care you don't burn yourself. Well done. Can you mix this cake?' she asked. 'I'll measure out the next two or three. It makes such a difference when there's two of us working.'

'Good.' Meg washed her hands again, then began to mix the flour and fruits — the kind of work she loved, but seldom did back home. There was little call for baking when you were living on your own.

'Wonder when he's going back to work,' mused Jo.

'Robert? He's hoping to sneak a week to ten days away from his office.'

'Mmm.' Jo weighed ingredients with more care than was necessary.

'This recipe for your fruitcake,' Meg said. 'Where did you get it?'

'At my grandma's apron strings. She had a floral apron that she wound round and round herself, then it was tied at the waist by tapes. As a child, I never saw her in anything else.'

'My gran too. It was a badge of honour for

that generation of women, something they wore from when they rose until they went to bed. They were slaves to their houses and their families.'

'Some things never change,' Jo said wryly.

'Oops, I've done it again,' Meg laughed. 'Opened my mouth and put my foot in it. How long have you been doing this — the baking and dog-walking?'

'Ever since I had to — to stay sane, as well as making ends meet. I'd no real choice. Seven years.' Jo worked her dough.

Meg checked the scones. 'They're doing nicely. And have you never had a break, a proper break . . . a holiday.'

'Using what for money?' Jo asked drily.

Meg frowned at the oven. She could wave a magic wand, but she knew that Jo would never accept the cash. Even to offer might cost her a friend.

'Don't even think it,' Jo said quietly, reading the pause

'I wouldn't insult you.'

Jo straightened wearily. 'These scones will be ready in five minutes,' she said. 'I want the oven to cool down a bit, before we put in the cakes. One of these days, it's going to blow up in my face. What would you say to a cup of tea?'

'I'd say we've probably earned it,' Meg replied.

'Good. Well, you're nearest the kettle.'

'Right, boss,' said Meg.

★   ★   ★

Andy Morris finished smoothing fresh plaster over where he had replaced a rotting window frame, and stood back to admire his work.

'You've missed a bit.'

He jumped as if shot, and saw Meg's head peering across the floorboards from the stairs. 'How did you get there?' he demanded.

'I sneaked in,' she said. 'Convinced you were sleeping in my time, because you were so quiet.'

'That silence was pure Yorkshire concentration,' he said solemnly. 'It comes expensive. What are you wanting, anyway?'

Meg climbed the remaining stairs from the old bakery. 'I didn't come back from Edinburgh to watch other people work. What can I do to help?'

Andy studied her. 'Are you serious?' he demanded.

'Absolutely — I hate doing nothing. Helping out will fill in the time for me, and it might just get the mill ready to stay in a bit quicker.'

She meant it, Andy decided, and Meg went up another few notches in his reckoning. 'We

112

can't do anything much inside until this plaster dries,' he said slowly. 'Both here and where I've patched up the rewiring. I was going outside, while the weather's good, to replace a couple of panes of glass. Then I need to finish repointing the weather side — that's replacing mortar between the rows of stones, to you. There's two ladders in the truck. If I showed you what to do, you could howk out the loose mortar for me. That would save time. And if you're still fit and willing, I can show you how to mix cement, and keep me going, while I finish off the pointing. That's a full day's work.'

'Good,' said Meg. 'Where do I start?'

'By making tea.'

'I brought a thermos flask. And milk and sugar.'

Andy stood, plaster-whitened hands on hips, admiration on his face. 'Eee, lass,' he smiled. 'Tha's got t' makin's o' a decent wife.'

'In your dreams,' she replied, with a grin.

'Nay, I were thinkin' o' tekkin' thee on as labourer.'

'Don't go all Yorkshire on me,' she said. 'I want a decent wage.'

Andy clutched his chest. 'Doan't mention words lik' that,' he groaned.

'What words?'

'Wages. We've burned men at t' stake for less.'

The blue eyes sparkled, and Meg's morning warmed and opened out as though from a blast of summer sun. 'I'll get my thermos,' she said. 'I left it downstairs. I suppose you've a mug hidden away?'

'With my full emergency pack,' he said. 'Knife, fork, spoon and bow tie, in case I'm invited out for a meal. And an old kettle and an even older primus stove out in t' truck, just in case I have to mek' do myself.'

'Well, you can leave aside your bow tie this time,' she said.

★   ★   ★

Their sniping started as the kind of sibling bickering that happened half a dozen times most days. Jo listened wearily, trying to sort out what had really happened and who, if anybody, was to blame. It would have defeated Solomon.

Her eyes picked out the tall figure of Robert Matthews, striding easily along the Kirkbymoorside pavement, heading back to his hotel. Her heart lifted; here was somebody who didn't seem to live in a round of perpetual squabbling.

'That's right!' she protested. 'Walk past me.'

Matthews stopped in his tracks, a slow

114

smile spreading over his face.

'I'm so used to seeing you with dogs,' he apologized.

'Trust me, dogs are easier to control,' Jo said with feeling. 'Robert, these are my kids, Anna and Jamie. And this is Robert Matthews, the London lawyer who is Meg's friend. You remember Meg, don't you?'

The girl smiled uncertainly. The young lad stared at Matthews.

'Hi,' said Robert. 'I've heard a lot about you both from your mum.'

'Don't listen to her,' Anna said. 'She's biased.'

Matthews laughed. 'It's always nice things that she says about you both — that's the best kind of bias in a mum.'

Jo felt herself blushing. Daft. 'Where have you been today?' she asked hastily, trying to divert the unaccustomed praise.

'Rievaulx Abbey and the Terraces. I walked a bit of the Cleveland Way as well. Stunning countryside. I'm seriously thinking of opening a branch of the business in Helmsley, and appointing myself as its manager — but that would be a gross abuse of power.'

'I've heard of the Terraces,' said Jo. 'But I've never been there.'

'I know, because you're too busy,' he said.

'Busy looking after this pair at my side. You should have joined us sooner — this is the quietest they've been all day.'

'Not true!' protested Anna.

'Where are you planning to go tomorrow?' Jo asked. 'Have you been to Whitby yet? Or taken the steam train from Pickering up to the North Moors.'

Matthews sighed. 'My plans have been scrapped. I got a phone call from the office this morning. There's an emergency meeting for all senior staff tomorrow night, and I must be there to chair it.'

'That's a shame!' exclaimed Jo. 'You had only just started your holiday.'

'And I have every intention of finishing it. But not until we have sorted out how to handle a new problem that has been dumped on our laps. Oh, the joys of being corporate lawyers and inheriting a botched-up deal! We need to get our heads round the problem, try a bit of horse-trading behind the scenes, and if it goes to court decide our best defence, then hire a barrister to tell lies for us.'

'Doesn't sound a bit like television lawyers,' said Anna. 'They always root around until they find the truth.'

'That's all very well in fiction,' Matthews grinned. 'In the business world truth is usually the first thing to be jettisoned. By both sides. So it's all about wheeling and dealing, and protecting one set of baddies from the other.'

'Then this is your last night here?' Jo asked. For no reason, she felt acutely disappointed.

'Until I can escape and come back.'

'Will you be having a last dinner with Meg tonight?'

'Perhaps. I haven't seen her all day.'

'She was going over to see if she could help Andy at the mill.'

Matthews shook his head admiringly. 'She's not one to let grass grow beneath her feet. Why don't you join us for dinner?'

'I can't,' said Jo. 'Not with these.' She nodded towards her teenagers.

'Bring them with you,' Matthews replied.

'I can't possibly. The dogs are better house-trained.'

'Mum!' Anna exclaimed.

Matthews laughed. 'Of course you can bring them. The more the merrier.'

Jo frowned. 'I know,' she said, 'why don't you both come out to me, and I'll cook dinner? How about that?'

Matthews hesitated, acutely aware that her money was tight.

'It's years since I've had people home for dinner,' Jo pleaded.

'Go on,' said Anna. 'We can leave him up in his room, to sulk.'

Matthews's smile died, as he turned to meet the boy's sullen gaze.

'I'm taking your silence as yes,' Jo said firmly. 'Be there at seven.'

★ ★ ★

Meg wearily filled her builder's hod with the last of the cement she had been mixing. Lifting it on to her right shoulder, she gripped the ladder and began the short climb with muscles which were on fire. What had started as fun had driven her to the edge of exhaustion. She climbed doggedly up.

Andy transferred her cement to his own plasterer's tray, glancing at her and reading both the weariness in and the steel beneath her dogged expression. A woman to value, he thought, good-humoured, steady and uncomplaining. 'With you helping, we've done two days' work,' he complimented her.

Meg glanced across. 'Honestly?'

'Honestly. Give me a couple of minutes to finish, and I'll get some water from the stream to wash our stuff. Never let cement set on any working tool.'

'Will I take my ladder down?' she asked.

'Leave it. There's an art to it.'

She watched him working methodically, then smoothing off the new mortar with the blunt end of his trowel, matching the slightly hollowed finish on the original. An artist, this man, she thought.

With trembling legs she descended to ground level.

'There's more plaster on me than on the mill,' she said.

'You've done just great.' The ladder creaked as he came down it. 'Another couple of days,' he said.

Meg brightened. 'Until I get in?'

'That's right. You still won't have electricity — the boys have promised to renew the old cable down to the road next week. But everything else you need will be working.'

'Great!' she said. At last, unable to stop herself, she leaned down to massage her leg muscles.

'You're going to suffer tomorrow. You should have stopped after a couple of hours, like I told you to.'

'It's my home. I want to work on it.'

Andy smiled. One feisty, stubborn lady, this. 'I've been thinking. We've saved a day — why not use it to look for your new furniture tomorrow?'

'Where?'

'There's places in Malton and Pickering, bigger dealers in Knaresborough and York. But I reckon you can get all you need within twenty miles of here.'

Meg ached to sit down, to take the weight off her legs.

'Can you give me some addresses?' she asked.

'Nay lass,' he said. 'I can do better than that. The only way for you to get a decent price is to set Yorkshireman against Yorkshireman. I was planning to take you round the dealers. By way of saying thanks, for the help you gave today. Deal?'

Meg swallowed. 'Deal,' she said, huskily.

* * *

'Come in,' said Jo. 'Where's Meg?'

'She sends her apologies,' replied Matthews. 'She's been working all day, helping out Morris at the mill. She's exhausted. She says she's going to soak in a bath for an hour at least, then grab a sandwich from the bar and go to bed.'

Jo closed the door. 'She's not afraid of hard work,' she said. 'She was up here last night, giving me a hand with the baking. We got it done in half the time.'

Matthews stood awkwardly in the small hallway, fighting the feeling of being an intruder. 'I know,' he said. 'I've never asked, and she has never told me, but I think she's had things pretty hard in life.'

Haven't we all, Jo thought bitterly. 'Come through and sit down,' she said, slightly

120

flustered at being left alone with Matthews. She'd been banking on Meg to help keep the conversation flowing over dinner. 'I hope you like chicken,' she added as they went through into the small lounge/dining room. Catering on a tight budget, she had gone for a couple of chickens, thinking that what wasn't eaten tonight would help out foodwise for a couple of days.

'Chicken? Great,' said Matthews, holding out a bottle of wine. 'I managed to find a New Zealand white. Freshen it in your fridge for twenty minutes, and we can have it with the meal.'

As she went into the kitchen with the wine, he looked round the walls; there were lots of photos, as there had been in the hall. Their common feature was the tall and smiling figure at the centre of most of them. Even at this distance, Matthews could feel the hard soldier's eyes behind the smile drill into him. It wasn't a comfortable sensation. His neck hairs tingled.

Jo came back, wiping her hands. 'Sit down,' she said, pulling out a chair at the head of the set table. 'Dinner's nearly ready — I'll give the kids a shout.

He heard her voice calling up the stairs of the small terraced house. A girl's voice answered. Footsteps running lightly down the stairs, then the door opened and the girl came in.

'Hello. Been doing your homework?' he asked.

She nodded. 'Latin,' she replied. 'It's a rubbish subject — why do they want to teach us a dead language in the twenty-first century?'

'You'd be surprised,' Matthews assured her. 'Botanists need to know it, because all their species carry Latin names. Doctors and chemists use it. And we lawyers would scarcely manage a day's work without it.'

'Do you understand Latin?' she asked, her interest suddenly aroused.

'A bit.'

'Hold on . . . ' She hurtled up the stairs and came back with a textbook and notebook. 'Translation,' she said. 'I've bogged down — can you help me out?'

'I'll try,' said Matthews, taking the textbook. 'Where's the problem?'

'Here . . . ' She ran her finger along the text. 'It's something that the guy's slave does, but I'm lost.'

Matthews struggled to remember schoolboy Latin, so different from the dry and precise legal terms. 'I think it's saying that the slave will light the tapers,' he said slowly. 'That's the wicks they burned in vases filled with oil, before anybody had candles.'

'I got some of the light bit,' Anna muttered. 'But what comes next?'

The two heads drew close together, poring over the page. 'That's sandal, I think,' said Matthews. 'I've got it! 'Once he lights the tapers, a slave will take off their sandals and wash their feet.''

'But why? What's he doing that for?'

'Think back,' Matthews said. 'A warm country, open sandals, dust and dirt . . . sweaty feet. Reclining sofas. Any hostess would want her guest's feet washed before she let them loll back on her best furniture.'

'Mum would go ballistic,' Anna agreed, scribbling feverishly.

Jo came through. 'What are you doing?' she asked. 'And where's Jamie?'

'Homework . . . and don't know,' said Anna. 'Yes I do — he's up in his room, and he's been grumpy all day. Boys . . . ' There was withering scorn in her voice.

'I'm just about to dish up. Go and get him for me, please.'

Anna looked indignantly at her new homework assistant.

'Why is it always me?' she demanded. 'Am I . . . like . . . a slave?'

'If you are you might have to wash his feet,' warned Matthews.

'Gross!' Anna hurtled out of the room and

thundered up the stairs.

Jo looked blankly at Matthews. 'What are you talking about?' she asked.

'Relax. It's something from her homework. Translation.'

'Oh,' Jo said. 'She's got you roped in already?'

'I've shot my bolt,' he admitted. 'Used up all my Latin.'

More footsteps sounded on the stairs, then Jamie was pushed through the door by his sister. He stood, frowning, over its threshold with that same cold stare fixed on Matthews, his eyes so like the older eyes in the photographs of his father.

'Why is he sitting in that chair?' he demanded. 'That's my dad's chair. He has no right to be sitting there.'

'Jamie!' exclaimed Jo, then the searing pain which his words had brought to her, sharpened her tongue. 'Well, your dad's not here any more, and he's not going to sit in it again!' she said tightly. 'So either we let the dust pile high in it, or use it as best we can.'

Jamie looked at her, as if she'd struck him across the face. At his back, Anna's hand rose to cover her mouth, her shocked eyes staring at her mother.

'Hold on,' Matthews said quietly, rising. 'Here, Jamie, you sit at the head of the table.

That should be your rightful place, a great honour, and an even bigger responsibility.' He pulled out a chair from the side of the table. 'I'll feel more comfortable down here.'

He seated himself. 'Let's get started,' he said. 'I'm famished.'

★　★　★

'Right,' said Andy. 'There are three types of dealers. One specializes in quality antique furniture — if you have to ask the price, you can't afford it. The second has decent old furniture, without hidden drawers and family jewellery. And the third specialises in repossessions — modern furniture where folk have fallen behind in their finance payments. Which do you want?'

'The second,' said Meg.

'I thought so. Now, for that, do you want a dealer who will swear that any woodworm holes are sixty years old at least, or a man who will check for and treat any infestations? Then add the cost to his price, but give you a guarantee?'

'Do you really need to ask?' Meg replied. 'Is that why we've drawn up here, outside Steptoe's yard? Tell me, have you chosen my actual furniture yet?'

Andy grinned. 'Nay lass,' he said. 'It would

be a brave man who chose a woman's furniture. I was nobbut trying to save us both some time. Old Harry is as honest as they come — for Yorkshire, anyway. That means he'd make a corkscrew look straight, but he stocks some good stuff, and he owes me a favour.'

'Because you brought some other trusting Scotswoman here before?'

'Close,' he admitted. 'But she came from Lancashire.'

'And went away penniless?'

'Penniless, but happy.' He climbed out of his truck and looked back, his blue eyes twinkling as he enjoyed the verbal sparring. 'Well . . . are you coming, or will we fetch stuff out to you?'

'Give me time,' Meg said, climbing stiffly out of the cab. All that work the day before had left every muscle aching, and every joint feeling full of grit.

Andy took her gently by the elbow and steered her through trestle-tables of pots and pans, vases and ancient china. 'Word in your ear,' he said quietly, without any trace of Yorkshire. 'Buy oak if you can — that's early 1900s. It will be in character with the rest of the mill, it's solid, and they never built better furniture. Harry has some stuff here from old houses up in the dales. Authentic. Will last for ever. And since oak's gone out of fashion, we can ask for a good price. He keeps his best stuff round the back. Let's see what he's got, then you can make up your mind.'

He knocked on the office door. 'Is he back yet?' he demanded. 'Or has the silly owld beggar gone to sleep in t' pub?'

'Less lip,' replied an older man's voice. 'I don't know what you're looking for, but I sold it yesterday. Go away — I'm busy.'

The door opened and an ancient stepped outside. Grey stubble sprouted on a grey face and his eyes were as washed out as any sailorman's. His gaze flicked to Meg and, she would have sworn, slipped inside her purse to check the state of her bank balance. 'Tha's in bad company, lass. I doan't know what he said about me, but it's lies.'

'He said you were the best dealer in old furniture that didn't cost a fortune.'

'Then he were drunk.' The washed-out eyes crinkled. 'Never tell a Yorkshire dealer he's the best — he'll only raise his price, to tek' advantage.'

'He said the rest would rip me off, but you were nearly honest.'

Harry laughed outright. 'That's more like it,' he chortled. 'What's tha lookin' for, lass?'

'Just about everything,' said Meg, with a sigh.

'Then tha's come to t' right place.' Meg found her elbow gently gripped for the second time that day, as she was steered through the yard's collection of rusting lawnmowers, weathered spades, tools from trades that had died out sixty years before, towards two large sheds at the furthest end. 'Now, do you want to start in t' kitchen, or in t' bedroom section?'

'Sections?' demanded Andy. 'Where stuff's left in heaps, more like.'

Meg swallowed. It took a lot of getting used to, having enough money now to do more or less as she pleased. She would adjust. In time. Meanwhile, she would do what she knew best: stick to tried and trusted principles.

'Whichever's cheapest,' she said.

Harry stopped in his tracks and turned to Andy.

'Eee, lad,' he said. 'If I were single, then I'd marry her on t' spot!'

★ ★ ★

High in his London office, Robert Matthews stood looking out across the City and its busy streets. His neat suit felt like a prison uniform. Apt. He was a prisoner now, in surroundings more familiar to him than his home, an austere and elegantly furnished

128

Chelsea flat. Worse, he was a prisoner in a life he no longer wanted.

What did he want? Was it simply the lure of a big Yorkshire sky, and the feel of the wind in his face? The feeling of being part of, and at peace with, the vast moorland landscape which stretched to every horizon around him? To some extent. But one could not stay on holiday for ever — even the most wonderful place and experience soon palls.

Was it the woman? Jo? With her strong face, her endlessly busy life as she struggled to cope, and her vulnerable eyes? In his mind he saw them now, reflecting the hurt and shock in the eyes of her children.

He had, by his presence there, caused that hurt.

Matthews's head drooped. Above him, his father's old wall clock ticked slowly.

There was a discreet knock on his office door.

'Yes?' he said, straightening up and walking over to his desk.

'Mr Matthews?' Alison, his loyal and dedicated secretary, without whom he would have been lost, came in to the room. At a glance, she read his face, noting the sadness at odds with the sunburn. Something's wrong in his life, she thought. Badly wrong.

'The others are waiting for you to chair the

meeting,' she said.

'Of course,' he replied. 'We mustn't disappoint them . . . '

* * *

'My goodness!' exclaimed Jo. 'What a transformation!'

She looked around the newly furnished middle floor of the mill, where dark oak furniture stood as if it had been there for generations: comfortable armchairs and a long settee; bookshelves; a dresser, cunningly placed to create a room divider from the dining room/kitchen. Thick old rugs were scattered on the wooden floor.

'You've even hung curtains,' Jo said. 'And the glow from these two paraffin lamps makes the whole place look like something out of *Ideal Home.*'

'It doesn't smell like *Ideal Home,*' Meg said ruefully. 'Every whiff is of other people's rugs and furniture — the curtains are the only new things here. This is the only room that's been finished. I'll have to bunk down here as well.'

'Don't worry about the smell,' said Jo. 'An afternoon washing down and polishing the furniture, a quick shampoo of your rugs . . . we'll soon chase that stink of showrooms.'

Meg noted the 'we', and swallowed. In the last few weeks down here, as a stranger, she had made more friends than in twenty years of living in Edinburgh. 'Thanks,' she said.

'When did all this happen?'

'Today. Andy helped me buy the stuff this morning. Then he and old Harry brought it up the track this afternoon — and we took turns at lugging it up the stairs. Did they have to make that old furniture so heavy!'

'It was built to last,' said Jo. 'Where's Andy?'

'Gone for a pint with Harry. The two of them cursed each other up hill and down dale all day — it was like World War III breaking out.'

Jo smiled. 'That's just two Yorkshire blokes who like each other. It's when they go quiet and stop complaining that you know there's aggro.' She walked into the lounge and sank into an armchair. 'Aaahhhh,' she sighed. 'Lovely. Here, this is yours.'

'What is?' Meg took the proffered plastic bag.

'Some food,' said Jo. 'I brought you a wedge of our chicken and leek pie, and the makings of a salad. I knew you wouldn't have any electricity to cook.'

'I was going down to the King's Head later,' Meg said. She blinked back the sudden flow of tears. 'This is the first meal I will ever eat in my new home — and I'm glad it was you who brought it to me, Jo. How can I ever thank you?'

'Come on, lass! Don't cry on me!' Jo said uncomfortably. 'It's only leavings from the chicken we had yesterday — scarcely any of that was eaten.'

'Why? How did last night go? Robert was up and away to London this morning, long before I surfaced.'

Jo sank deeper into her armchair, feeling her tensions ease.

'A disaster,' she said bleakly. 'From start to finish.'

'How? Why?'

'Jamie started it. He was a pain, so rude. Robert tried to smooth things over — he's such a nice guy. But I bit off Jamie's head, and the three of us sat there, hating each other, while Robert tried to rescue the meal. I undid all the good he'd done in charming Anna by helping her do her Latin homework. Then I drank too much because I was so tense and embarrassed, and scarcely found a sensible thing to say. Anna got up halfway through the meal and went back upstairs. While Jamie just sat, playing with his food and staring across the table. It was the first time I've had anybody in . . . since Jim died, I suppose. And it couldn't have gone worse, shown what a dysfunctional family we've become. Then Robert apologized, said he'd an early start, and left us to it. A nightmare!'

'I'm so sorry,' Meg said. 'I was absolutely shattered . . . '

'You wouldn't have made any difference. It was total war, so far as Jamie was concerned. Will I light your fire, while you're serving up your dinner?'

'Please,' said Meg. 'I've been looking forward to that all day. My final step in turning this house into a home. Sorry, but I can't offer you wine — not even a cup of tea.'

'I've had all the wine I want to see,' Jo grimaced. 'As for tea, there's a thermos, down in my car. I'll get that while the fire is catching. I see you've got it set and ready to light.'

'All it needs is a match and an old-fashioned blessing.'

Jo reached on to the rough stone mantelpiece for the box of matches, then carefully sparked one and held it to the tail of rolled newspaper, which was poking out from between the logs. Kneeling, she watched the yellow flames lick up, catch in the small kindling at the heart of the fire, then spread to the sticks which were set in a pyramid above.

'Nothing beats a real fire,' she said quietly. 'I remember lighting my own first fire, when we were married.'

Meg waited, bag in hand; but Jo's voice drifted into silence. 'Can you think of a blessing for the fire and house?' Meg asked. 'It doesn't have to be religious, just something, to bring me luck. You're my friend, you've brought the first food into the house. Can you make a wish for me too?'

Jo blinked into the flames as they blurred before her eyes. Roughly, she scrubbed her face with the back of her hand.

'A blessing?' she said. 'Right. May this fire and this home bring you the same happiness that I knew. But may they also bring you a better ending.'

Meg knelt down, slipping an arm round her. 'I'll settle for that,' she said huskily. 'Only I want a better ending for you too.'

'Dream on,' said Jo.

6

Meg wakened to the sound of wind rustling over treetops, and the endless burbling of the river. She lay in her made-up bed on the sofa, relaxed and happy. It was early, far too early to get up. Drowsily, she listened as the first birds began to sing, then the whole birdsong chorus joined in. She fell asleep again and wakened later with a start.

Andy would be here to begin work at any time. She flew out of bed, wincing as her leg muscles protested, and began to wash in cold water. Aaarghhh! The shock woke her up, and left her skin zinging, her mind totally alert and alive.

She checked her watch: barely 7.30 a.m. In less of emergency mode she folded up the bedding and stowed it away, then tidied up the room and opened the windows even further to let in the day.

Leaning on the windowsill, she looked out. She loved this place.

Andy would be here around 8 a.m. she thought. She would hand over her mill to him, nip down through the woods for breakfast and a coffee, then come back to help as best she could. It was a nuisance, not having any electricity — and not being linked up to gas. He had offered her his primus, but his lesson on how to start the thing had seemed so complicated that she had opted for a cold-water start, then an early morning walk to get her breakfast.

She threw open the front door and breathed in keen air. Wonderful.

Leaving the door wide open, she turned back into the old bakery floor, and began to explore. It was the first time she'd been here on her own with time on her hands. She pushed through into the mysterious jumble of iron rods, chains and gears, which were the working part of the mill. Then came back to look thoughtfully at the bakery oven.

Tentatively, she tried to open the main iron door. The metal was thick with rust, its hinges solid. She tried a smaller door: same result. She was wrestling with it when a shadow loomed across the sunlit floor towards her.

'Hay-oop!' said Andy. 'What's this you're doing?'

'Trying to open the oven door.'

'You never mentioned getting them ready. Here, let me. Brute force and ignorance, the main contribution to civilization from the Yorkshire male . . . '

His calloused fingers struggled with the edge of the door.

'Needs modern technology,' he said. 'Hang on.'

He disappeared to his truck and came back with an aerosol. 'WD40 — an oil that penetrates all joints and makes mincemeat out of seized hinges. With this secret power, even I can look like Superman.'

'Without the cape?' Meg teased.

'Hang on! The cape costs time and a half.'

'We'll pass on the cape then.'

'Won't be easy, but I'll try.' Frowning, he squirted the oil liberally over the seized hinges. 'Give it a second to do its work,' he said. 'There's a thermos in my bag. Black coffee, I brought it up for you. There's milk and sugar too. And in the pack with greaseproof paper, there's a couple of bacon butties. Your breakfast. I thought they would taste better than kippers and toast.'

'For me?' Meg asked.

'They were,' he said. 'But if you hang around, I'll halve them with you.'

'No chance,' she said.

'Hope you like the HP sauce. It's the authentic Yorkshire touch.'

'Mmphmm,' Meg replied indistinctly.

Andy grinned. He couldn't stand a woman who picked at her food and was taking real pleasure from watching his bacon sandwiches disappear.

'Let's try again,' he said. There was a grating noise. 'Told you. There's your door open.' He peered inside. 'Hey. I think you've won a gold watch . . . let me try a couple of these other doors.' He worked busily with his aerosol.

'Why a gold watch?' Meg asked, then filled her mouth again.

Andy looked up. 'This is like an Aga cooker — a whole series of ovens, with different sizes and working temperatures. It's the Victorian range system that Aga copied.' He grinned. 'To get one of these new would cost you eight to ten thousand pounds, and this is an industrial size. You've got it for free.'

'But the rust?'

'Wire wool and elbow grease will get rid of it.'

'And the firebricks inside?'

'I'm going out for my torch, to check. From finger-feel, they seem sound.'

'So would it work?'

Andy puffed out his cheeks. 'Hey, it could be a hundred years since it was last fired. Or fifty — who knows.' He sat on his heels, deep in thought. 'If the bricks and mortar are still sound . . . if there's no cracks in the firebox . . . if we could find a way of sweeping the chimney . . . '

He looked up. 'In theory, yes it could still

work if it's undamaged. In practice, you'd only find out by lighting the fire.'

'What would it burn?'

'Wood or coal,' he said. 'Probably wood originally, given the amount of land under forestry here and up north. Why are you asking all these questions? You have a perfectly good log fire and a chimney that I swept myself, upstairs.'

Meg frowned. 'I'm not really sure,' she said slowly. 'Yes, I am. If I could get this working properly, then it could be the bigger oven that Jo wants so badly and can't afford.'

'Baking for the markets?'

'Yes. How long would it take, to check it out?'

'How long is a piece of string? If it's sound, a day or so to check and sweep, and clean. If bricks or chimney wall is cracked, a couple of months and a major rise in costs. Your lawyer friend would never allow it. And if he did, I wouldn't.'

Meg knelt down and peered into the dark oven. 'It's huge,' she said.

'And that's one of the smaller ovens. It's bread, not scones, that this was built to make. The mill would grind its own flour, then bake for the village.'

'Mmm,' said Meg. 'Is there anything urgent that needs to be done to the mill — or could we use a couple of days to check and clean out the oven? And, if we hit any major problems . . . just close it up again, and get on with the house?'

Andy rose smoothly. 'It's your money,' he said.

'And my decision. OK, let's do it.'

'I'll get my torch,' said Andy.

★ ★ ★

Jo struggled into the mill, her hands full of pails and mops. 'I brought my own stuff over,' she said. 'I wasn't sure what you'd have . . . what are you two doing? Is there something wrong?'

Meg turned from holding the torch for Andy, who was halfway inside one of the medium ovens. 'Wrong? No, it could be that there's something right.'

'What do you mean?' asked Jo, setting down her cleaning materials.

'This old bakery oven . . . Andy thinks it's still usable.'

'Hey! Concentrate on pointing that torch,' came Andy's muffled voice from inside the oven. 'More to the left. That's it.'

Jo came uncertainly over. 'Usable? What for?'

'Just a minute,' said Meg. 'Or you'll get me

into trouble again.'

'No. I need to come out for a breather,' Andy said, reversing out.

Jo smiled. 'You have soot or stuff, all over your face. You're like a minstrel.'

He grinned. 'Worth it. That's three of the ovens we've checked out, and they're filthy but the bricks and mortar seem to be as good as the day they last worked. That leaves only the main oven to do. I think I'll sweep that out, and check it properly. If it's in good shape, then it's all down to the firebox and its chimney.'

'What is?' Jo demanded. 'Your face is filthy too.' This last was directed at Meg, who had just rubbed a dirty hand across eyes which were itching from ancient dust, and was looking like a panda.

'Who cares,' Meg said cheerfully. 'I think — just *think* at this stage, mind you — that we have solved your oven problem. There is a huge baking space in here, enough for double what you're doing right now — even more. Andy says it's like an Aga cooker, with different temperatures in the different ovens. You'll be able to bake almost everything at once.'

Jo looked from one to the other. 'But it's a hundred years old, if it's a day.'

'If it's still in working order, does that matter?'

'It's filthy.'

'So we clean it, and worry about the room upstairs later.'

Andy coughed. 'Hey! Hold your horses. No point in cleaning until I suss out how to get the chimney swept. Lord only knows what's jammed in there — or if it's still open, for air to get in and smoke to get out.'

'Everything else is working, so why not that? It looks to me like they simply stopped baking, then left a perfectly good oven to rust away.' Meg rubbed at a rusty oven door. 'But this would take centuries to destroy. So I think we have a winner. Where will we get wire wool? That's what you said we needed, wasn't it?'

Andy solemnly made a T with his two hands. 'I'm calling a time-out. We're running, before we've learned to walk. Why don't you two go and scrub clean whatever it was that Jo came over to do with you . . . and leave me to figure out how to check the firebox and the flue.'

'But this is more exciting,' protested Meg.

'Give me an hour,' he said. 'Two hours. Otherwise we'll all be getting jammed in the same oven door, in each other's way.'

'If you insist,' grumbled Meg. She turned to Jo. 'What do you think?'

Jo was staring at the ancient bakery, her

mind racing. She came back to the present, with a start. 'I think this is all too good to be true. And when something seems too good to be true, it generally is . . . '

'Am I the only optimist among you?' Meg demanded.

'No,' said Jo. 'But some of us know there can be mirages too.'

★　★　★

High in his London office, Matthews massaged his eyes with his fingertips. The morning rush hour was still building in the City streets below. How often had he sat here, in before everyone else, sharing the empty City with fellow insomniacs like commodity traders? They at least were making money. He was here because he had nothing better to do. A condemnation, surely, on his life.

He sighed and pulled a file of papers towards him. Once the job, and the challenges of running his father's firm, had been enough. Not quite true. It had helped to keep him sane, after losing Nancy and their daughter Gemma. The job itself was no more than a substitute for life, if the truth be told, and necessary because people were depending on him.

He flipped through the papers, frowning in

concentration. Then pulled a pad towards himself and began to write, referring back to the documents from time to time. Slowly, he became absorbed, and the clock speeded up on the wall above him, while the noise of traffic grew on the street outside. He never noticed.

His concentration was disrupted by a discreet knock on his door.

'Alison? Come in,' he called. 'You're early today.'

Not as early as he habitually was, she thought. 'Would you like to check through your meetings for this morning, Mr Matthews?' she asked.

'Please do,' he said.

'You have Mr Sutton at 9.30 on the Broadstairs case. Miss Howton at 10.00, to talk through the executory issues she's facing. Then Mr Oldham, to check how things are moving on his case at 11.00. Then a working lunch at 12.00, with the other senior partners.'

'Have you booked a table?'

'Of course. Then there's Mr Boothby at 1.15 . . . '

'How is young Marcus settling in?' Matthews asked.

Alison hesitated, aware that any information request was always for a good purpose, and would be treated as strictly confidential.

'The girls say he's pretty good,' she said. 'Knows his law, knows when to ask for advice, has a nice manner with his clients, gets on well with office staff.'

'Hmm.' Matthews frowned: 'the girls' were the senior secretarial Mafia, the inner core of long-serving women who held everything together. Knew more about what was going on and where the likely weaknesses lay, than did the partners.

'How do you spell delegation, Alison?' he asked.

Accustomed to his wry sense of humour, she smiled. 'How would you spell it, Mr Matthews?' she countered.

'Let's see. B — O — O — T — H — B — Y, I think.'

'Indeed?' She waited patiently.

Matthews spun his office chair to look out through his office window.

'I've been thinking,' he said. 'If I ran away and joined the Foreign Legion, this whole place would stagger and collapse in its tracks.'

'I don't think there is a Foreign Legion any more . . . '

'Then it's time somebody restarted it. And put in place the necessary training here. It's downright dangerous, when an organization becomes so dependent on a single man. Tell

145

Marcus that I want to see him for twenty minutes, after we deal with his cases.'

'Yes, Mr Matthews.' Alison jotted down a quick note.

'Am I right in thinking that there's nothing too major in the week ahead?' he asked. 'Nothing that can't be postponed?'

Her mind skimmed over the calendar on her desk. 'Not until next week,' she said. 'Then there's the supermarket court case coming up. Mr Frenshaw will want to talk that through with you.'

'Adrian can help him,' said Matthews. 'It's time the whole place got used to working through ten days without me.'

'Thank goodness,' she said, before she could stop herself.

Matthews revolved his chair slowly back. 'Has it been that bad?'

'Not at all,' she said, blushing.

'Have I become the old grey ogre, who haunts the top floor of the building?'

Alison took a deep breath, her loyalty to and liking of her boss pushing her into taking a step she might regret later. 'Not yet,' she answered. 'I would say you're just the tired old man, who is only half the age he looks.'

'Wow!' he said, smiling. 'That good?'

In for a penny, in for a pound, she thought. 'We will — all of us here — heave a sigh of

146

relief if you run away to your Foreign Legion for a week, or a fortnight. Your choice. To put it right.'

'Put what right?'

'Whatever's bothering you.'

Flustered, but defiant, she gripped her notepad.

Matthews studied his secretary: a quiet and steady woman who had dedicated herself to her job, and caring for an elderly mother. Not once, so far as he knew, had there been a hint of romance — or restlessness — in her life. With her understated competence, she was as important to the firm as he was. 'Alison,' he said. 'I think it's time we increased your salary.'

'But you can't,' she protested. 'You increased it only four months ago.'

'Tough,' said Matthews. 'As of now, it is increased again.'

★　★　★

'Have you any idea how you look?' demanded Meg.

Andy grinned, teeth white against a soot-blackened face. 'Like the chimney sweep from Mary Poppins. Only he can dance a whole lot better than me.'

'Dick Van Dyke is almost a hundred years

old by now,' she said with a laugh.

'Trust me — he still dances better than me.'

'Will the chimney work?' asked Jo.

Andy nodded. 'By some miracle there's no blockage. But there might be cracks in the brickwork. We won't know until we light the fire.'

'What happens if there are cracks?' asked Meg.

'I don't want to think about that — not with half the mill already done.'

She stared at him. 'Is it a fire risk?'

With filthy hands he scratched his filthy hair. 'Don't think so,' he said after a bit. 'At worst, there could be some smoke seeping through. The rest of the heating system is in good nick, so the chimney is probably fine. You may get some loose soot flaring — that's a chimney-on-fire to you.'

'What do we do if that happens?'

'Let it burn itself out. In the old days, people used to set their chimneys on fire deliberately, to save on paying a sweep. One in a thousand, maybe even ten thousand, had so much soot to burn that the chimney bricks went red hot, and the fire brigade had to be called in. And the mess they made, pouring water down the chimney, cost a whole lot more than your average sweep.'

'How worried should we be?'

'On a scale of one to ten, probably one. The flue has already been scraped and swept. There can't be any major deposits of loose dry soot left — more likely caked wet soot. That won't burn.' Andy gathered the four corners of his dustsheet containing the soot, and knotted them tight. 'Let me get rid of this while you're cleaning up,' he said. 'There will be soot everywhere — sorry, but it's the nature of the beast. When I come back, we'll set a minor fire. Then put on some green wood, and check the chimneybreast for leaks.'

As in most things he did and said, there was a quiet competence that gave you confidence. 'Thanks, Andy,' said Meg.

Jo glanced at her watch. 'I've got to run, Meg,' she said. 'Two dogs to walk, then the kids to pick up. It will be night before I'm free again — and then I'm baking. Will you be coming over?'

'I'll be here,' said Meg. 'Once I get this clean, I want to nip into the village and buy some baking stuff.'

'To try out the oven?'

Meg nodded.

'That should be me,' Jo said uncomfortably.

'Not tonight,' said Meg. 'I've got to sort out how the whole system works — which ovens are hot and which cooler. There are no temperature gauges.'

'They worked from experience,' said Andy. 'Knowing when to stoke up the fire, and when to let it die back a bit.'

'And how do I get that experience?' Meg asked wryly.

'Don't ask me. I'm just the sweep.'

'Trial and error,' Jo muttered. 'I want to come over here, and do the baking. But I can't. It has to be perfect for the market . . . I need that money. I can't take the risk of ruining everything. Or doing it wrong.'

'No need,' said Meg determinedly. 'Let me play around with it tonight, and see if I can suss out how it works.'

'There's always Old Fred,' said Andy, still in the doorway.

'Who's Old Fred?'

'He used to work in a bakery, over in Pickering. It was an old family bakery, probably using ovens not much different from this. He's knocking on a bit, but if he's fit enough, I can ask him to come over and show you how this works.'

'Is there anybody around here that you don't know?' Meg demanded.

White teeth flashed. 'There must be one or two,' he admitted. 'But I'll tell 'ee this, lass. If I doan't know thim, then they've nivver owed me owt.'

'Stop going all Yorkshire on me!' Meg laughed.

She turned to Jo. 'Away and get on with your dog-walking. Leave me to clean up here. When Andy comes back, we'll set a low fire and check things out. If there are no leaks, then I will make up some dough and try some scones tonight. If they're a disaster, no problem — you'll have your own baking to take to the market tomorrow. But if they're half-decent, I'll bring them over and you can have a look at them. Then maybe we can do half at your place, and half here, next time. And if that works out, maybe we can try the entire lot here, next week.'

Jo nodded. 'That would be great. Thanks,' she said awkwardly.

'Too soon,' said Meg. 'Let's wait and see how things turn out.'

★　★　★

Jo had made up her three-times-weekly baking order for baking for so many years, that she could have done it on automatic pilot. But she worked steady and methodically through it all. In baking, as in theatre, you are as good as your last performance.

Part of her mind was on the old bakery in Meg's mill. Was that a red herring, a false dawn? Or was it really possible? Could the ancient bakery ovens be fired and brought back into useful life again? If so, it opened endless possibilities. But Jo had been hurt so badly once before in future planning that she had schooled herself to do exactly what the soldiers did, and simply watch where she was putting down each foot for its next step forward.

Meg's kindness was both heart-warming, and frightening. Jo had struggled for so long on her own that her independent state of mind was almost a given, round which she worked everything else in her life. She was alone. Of course her kids loved her — even if they hid it well, most days. But no one else had taken the time to befriend her and ask what she was doing, then been thoughtful enough to try and come up with a way to help her out.

It had been so long since anyone had held out a helping hand that she found it difficult to know how to react. That was where the frightening bit came in: what was going to happen if she let other people come into her lonely life? What if she became dependent on them? Grew weak?

She had two teenage kids to rear, and must stay strong. The problems that were already facing her in handling their future were overwhelming. If she lost her inner strength, the native resourcefulness, which had carried them this far as a family, then she was done for; they all were. That was a scary thought indeed.

Should she go with the flow and take the friendly hand which Meg was offering? Or should she find a way to distance herself, politely refuse? Stay as she was, becoming more tired and bitter with every year that passed. Watching time leave its footsteps across her face. Should she . . . ?

The lock on the gate to her back door clicked.

Jo stopped. It was 9 p.m. at least, she was too covered in flour to check. It must be Meg, she thought. Come round to show her the cindered remains of the pilot run of scones. She braced herself not to be disappointed. Even if the old bakery could be brought back to life, the two of them would have to learn how to work it. Common sense and experience. Therefore she must be positive, encouraging Meg, whatever disaster she was bringing over.

Dusting her hands on her apron, she walked to the door and opened it.

Then stepped back. 'What are you doing here?' she gasped.

In the light from the kitchen, Robert

Matthews stood on her doorstep.

'Taking the rest of my holiday,' he said wryly. 'I caught an afternoon train up from London. Managed to book a rental car again. Checked in at the King's Head, and grabbed a quick dinner. Then came out to see how you were . . . and to bring you these . . . '

From behind his back he brought out a small bunch of flowers and a beautifully wrapped and hugely expensive looking box of chocolates.

Jo found her voice. 'Hey,' she said quietly. 'I'm as old as the hills.'

'Me too.'

'Far too old to be impressed, by the likes of these.'

'I knew that.'

She studied him and, from somewhere dead inside her, a small spark of light appeared in what for years had been the densest darkness known to man — or woman. It was a light which flickered, blossomed, brightening up the night, slowly washing away the shadows of frustration, exhaustion, and residual grief.

'You're crazy, Robert,' she said.

'No. For the first time for years, I have seen sense.'

'It's all unknown. The kids . . . us . . . it's likely to end in tears.'

'Let's see if it does,' he said quietly. 'Rather

than back away, and wonder for the rest of our lives whether it might just have worked out.'

Jo hesitated only for a second. 'Come in,' she said. 'Or the scones will be ruined on me.'

'We daren't have that,' said Matthews.

He smiled and, like the light which still bloomed inside her, it brought back to life his quiet face, and made him young again.

'Are you any good with dough?' she demanded.

'Only one way to find out — as in life,' he replied.

★ ★ ★

'Have you eaten?'

Meg looked up wearily. 'No. Clearing up took a lot longer than I thought.'

'I guessed as much,' said Andy. 'Here. I've brought some food for you.'

'More bacon butties?' she raised a quizzical brow.

'Not much better,' he admitted. 'I'm a decent cook — really. But I had to get something that I could bring over to you cold. When I went home tonight I dropped in and bought a pork pie for us. You've never lived until you've tasted Vera's pies. And here's some cold potatoes and a bit of salad, to make a meal of it.'

Nothing is more powerful than simple kindness. Meg swallowed. 'How am I going to be able to afford this bill of yours, when it comes in?' she demanded.

'You can always pay it by instalments,' he replied. 'Have you lit the fire again, since we ran the test?'

'No. I was scared I would run out of wood.'

'Not a problem. Sit down and get that food inside you while I get the fire going. I spoke to Old Fred. He's up for it, and will be coming over tomorrow, to see what sort of old-fashioned oven you've got. Then show you how to use it.'

'Can he bake bread?' Meg asked, sitting wearily at the table and unwrapping cling film from the plate of salad. He'd put some slices of apple, red peppers, and small orange segments into the salad, she saw. A nice touch, giving it some zing.

'Bread? Probably. He was head baker for years in Pickering. Why?'

'Mmm. This pork pie is unbelievable,' Meg said through a large mouthful.

'Its recipe has come down through the Waind family for years. It's Vera's son who runs it now — but he still gets his mam to make the pies. Why this sudden interest in baking bread?'

'Just an idea I have.'

'Let's hear it,' Andy said, working away busily.

Meg looked longingly at her dinner. 'I haven't really taken time to think it through,' she said.

'I'll make allowances.'

Meg pushed the plate — and temptation — away.

'If I'm staying here,' she said, 'I'll have to find work. I'm not cut out to be a lady of leisure. I'll have used up most of the money anyway, in getting the mill house back to rights. So I'll need a job, and if it's the same down here as it is up north work's hard to get. So I was thinking of maybe setting up some kind of small business, something I could do . . . '

'And?' he said, as she gave into temptation and had another bite of pie.

'Mmphmm,' she replied indistinctly, and swallowed. 'At first, I only thought of these ovens as the answer to Jo's prayers. But the more I've worked on them today, the bigger I see they are. This is a commercial bakery — it could make far more scones and cakes than Jo could sell. But what if I expanded her cottage industry? What if we started baking home-made bread as well? Would that sell in the market? I don't know . . . but if it did, then we could run this place as a partnership.

157

Jo could give up all her other work, apart from baking. And I could work with her, do the paperwork, maybe even the marketing — it wouldn't be any more difficult than what I did before.'

Andy sat back on his heels.

'I know, I know,' she sighed, waving her hand. 'One step at a time.'

'We've still to ruin our first batch of scones,' he cautioned, but his eyes were twinkling. 'Get that food down you. I'm going down to the river to fetch up some pails of water.'

'Whatever for?' she asked.

'A serious fire is going to heat things up a lot more, than a small smoky one testing for cracks in the chimneybreast. I've some pails out in the truck.'

'Why are you doing all this?' she asked him quietly.

'All what?'

'Being there when I need you, looking after me . . . being so . . . nice?'

In the doorway he shrugged. 'I've got shares in you,' he said. 'You're my best customer. I need to keep you alive, until you pay the bill. And if you're going to build up the place into a full working bakery, then there's more building and repair work will have to be done. Anyway . . . ' His voice tailed off.

'Anyway, what?' she asked, her dinner forgotten.

'That's just it,' he said. 'Anyway is just a noise people make, when they run out of words or ideas.' He turned away into the dusk, then came back. 'Anyway,' he said sharply, 'haven't you a guy out there whose job it is to look after you?'

Meg shook her head. 'Nary a one,' she replied.

'Humph! Men up north must be blind, or daft, or both,' he growled. 'Near as bad as the folk from Lancashire.'

Meg was left staring at the rectangle of Yorkshire twilight. She was still staring, a slight smile on her lips, when he came clattering back, water slopping over the rims of two pails.

'Was that meant to be a compliment?' she demanded.

'Nay, lass. 'T were an observation. They come cheaper on t' bill.'

'I'm glad of that,' she said. 'But thanks.'

'Thank me by getting that grub down thee. We've bakin' to do,' he said.

7

Meg was still tidying up from the baking pilot run the night before, when there was a knock at the mill door. Probably Andy, back to start his morning's work.

'Come in!' she shouted.

The door opened, and sunlight streamed past two figures. One was unmistakably Andy, tall and broad-shouldered as ever. The other was much smaller, so frail that sunlight seemed to shine through him. Meg scrambled to her feet from the floor in front of the main oven.

'See what the cat brought in,' Andy said cheerfully.

'Cheeky beggar!' The bowed figure limped in, leaning heavily on a walking-stick. 'Young lads know nowt about respect for t' elderly,' he told her.

'This is Fred,' said Andy. 'What he doesn't know about baking wouldn't fill a decent sandwich. He's come to see your ovens.'

'She's nobbut a lass,' observed Fred. 'Good-looker, too.'

'I think that's you he's talking about,' Andy observed gravely. 'At his age, it might be the ovens.' His eyes sparkled.

Meg blushed furiously. Ridiculous.

'You baked them scones?' The oldster hobbled across the floor, heading for the tray of scones and pancakes.

'Last night,' said Meg. 'We were just experimenting.'

Fred picked up a scone, broke a piece off it and crumbled it between the fingers of his free hand, the other leaning heavily on his stick. 'She can bake, an' all,' he judged, then popped a crumb or two into his mouth and chewed noisily.

'Will I get some butter?' Meg asked.

'Nay lass,' he said. 'Needs pinch o' soda in it. But it'll do.'

He sniffed, rubbing the back of his hand across his nose.

'Pancakes too flat,' he said. 'Mixture needs more beatin'.'

Meg winced. She hadn't expected such a ruthless examination. 'We couldn't get the temperature right,' she explained. 'It's not like a normal oven.'

'Nay, 'tis better than normal oven. Served my apprenticeship on one of these — five years, lad, before they paid me decent wage.' This last was directed at Andy.

'You probably weren't worth one until then,' Andy replied.

'Cheeky beggar.' Fred turned slowly towards Meg. 'What's tha want t' bake for, lass? Theer's more than enough bakers in t' world that doan't know first thing about bakin'.'

From the gleam in his eye, she hoped he was winding her up.

'I want to help a friend who bakes for the local markets,' Meg said. 'Then I saw how big these ovens were, and wondered if we could maybe bake bread. Can you teach me how to do that? Just to bake small batches?'

'If tha tekks a tellin'. Few wimmen do.'

Meg smiled. 'I'd try my best.'

'Don't be taken in by her smile,' warned Andy. 'After what she said last night, when the first scones came out the oven . . . I'd say she's got a temper.'

Fred cackled. 'All the best o' thim has that.' He snorted. 'My old missus, she were half Irish — an' I'd have feared for meself if she'd been three-quarters Irish. She could light a fire at twenty yards, when she got goin'.'

'Don't listen to Andy.' Meg laughed. 'I'll be on my best behaviour.'

'Then I can teach thee. Is it modern bread tha wants t' mekk?'

She shook her head. 'Up in Edinburgh the bakeries doing best are the ones that have gone back to traditional methods. Their customers come from miles around — because their bread tastes like proper bread again. Can you do organic?'

The faded eyes twinkled. 'Eee, lass,' he said. 'When I were boy, it were all organic. We knew nowt else. All them insect killin' sprays, fert'lizers that mekk crops yield more, fancy yeasts that raise dough fast, an' chemical rubbish that keeps bread fresh for longer — they'd still to be invented. What we put int' bread was what t' Good Lord intended. Organic? I can teach thee how to mekk bread as it were allus made and had t' proper feel an' taste. Is that what tha wants?'

Meg nodded. 'And these ovens?'

Reversing his stick, Fred hooked open the main oven door.

'This fires well?' he asked of Andy.

'Like a dream.'

'Did tha burn wood, or coal?'

'Wood.'

Fred nodded. 'Easier to heat, an' better to control temperatures.'

Meg could wait no longer. 'How do you know what the temperatures are?'

Fred looked surprised. 'You just know,' he said. 'In old days, we used t' spit int' oven, and listen to it sizzle. A good sizzle tells 'ee better than any gauge.'

'We'll learn to judge without that,' Meg said firmly.

Andy grinned. 'What did I tell thee, Fred?' he said. 'About that temper?'

The old man nodded. 'I heard her,' he said. 'That were t' boss talking'.'

Meg blushed. 'When can you start teaching me?'

Fred scratched an elongated ear for a full minute. 'How about today?' he asked.

Meg gulped. 'But I don't have any flour, or tins or proper trays.'

'Tha's got car,' he said. 'I saw 'un, when Andy brought us in.'

'Are there shops where we can buy some bags of flour?' she asked.

'Bags? It's sacks tha needs. If we do this at all, we do't proper.'

'OK, sacks. Where do we get them.'

'Best flour's still in Thirsk,' he said. 'I worked wi' his gran'da.'

'What about baking tins and trays . . . ?' Meg was floundering.

Fred caught the lobe of his ear and stretched it improbably; it looked as if it was well used to this form of exercise.

'Why, lass,' he said mildly. 'Didn't I say? Tha can borrow mine.'

Meg looked desperately over to Andy for guidance. None came.

'I can pay you for them . . . ' she said hesitantly.

164

'Nay! I'm not sellin'.' The faded eyes twinkled. 'Hand 'em back t' me when tha's done wi' thim.'

Meg's eyes were held in his mild blue stare. If her idea worked, then she could be using his trays for longer than he might last himself. Then she saw the twinkle grow into a broad smile. He had got there first, making his offer in the full knowledge that he was probably making her a free gift of his gear.

All on the basis of ten minutes' acquaintance.

She stuck out her hand, felt it gripped with surprising — but restrained — strength. 'Deal,' she said. 'How can I ever thank you?'

Andy cleared his throat apologetically. 'I hope you realize that you're his apprentice now. Five years, following every whim and order. Before he pays you a decent wage.'

'I thought these words were banned in Yorkshire,' she said with a smile.

'Oh, they are,' he replied. 'So long as you remember that.'

★ ★ ★

'It's stupid, I know,' muttered Jo. 'But I still feel as if I'm cheating on Jim.'

'Likewise, on Nancy,' Matthews replied. 'Yet they'd both be the first to kick our

165

backsides into leaving the past behind, and moving on with our lives.'

Jo walked silently for a few steps, her head down. 'That's true,' she said at last. 'It's what I've told myself a hundred times — no, a thousand times — since I brought the kids here. In most things, you have no choice. Life goes on. But it's the personal stuff, your feelings. These never listen to reason, they clutter your mind, make you confused. So don't let's rush into this too fast, Robert, that would freak me out. I'm happy, really happy, for the first time in years. I don't want to risk losing that.'

It was a long speech, for her. The longest he had ever heard her make.

'Relax,' said Matthews. 'I feel the same. Let's take things like a long hard journey: one step at a time. I'm a walker and right now I'm walking through some lovely woods; that's step one. At my side is the woman I came back hundreds of miles, to see again and I'm happy. That's step two. Step three can wait.'

Jo smiled up at him. 'You're seriously weird. A man with sensitivity.'

'Anything but,' he protested, colouring.

'You should be a Scot — we can take anything but praise.' She gave a little laugh.

The path narrowed, bringing them closer together. His hand brushed hers, without his meaning it to. Before she knew what she was doing she had caught it and they were holding hands. She tried to make herself let go, and found that she couldn't.

'I think step three has just happened,' she said unsteadily.

'Good. I was trying to pluck up the courage,' he replied.

They walked on in silence for a few minutes, still close together although the path had broadened out again. 'I'd forgotten how much comfort you can draw from simple human contact,' she said quietly.

'Me too.'

The old dog stopped to sniff the roots of a tree. They stopped beside him, still holding hands.

'What are we going to say to Meg?' Jo asked.

Matthews smiled wryly. 'I don't think we'll need to say too much,' he replied. 'I think she's sussed us out already.'

Jo grimaced. 'She's sharp as a tack. Come on, Ben, your paws will grow roots, if we don't move on.' She glanced up at Matthews. 'There's a path along here we can take, if you want. It leads down to her mill.'

'Not yet,' said Matthews. 'I'm savouring the moment.' He coughed apologetically. 'You wouldn't, by any chance, know a longer way back home?'

Jo laughed. 'It's twenty years since anyone last asked me that. And the daft thing is, it makes me feel all young and bubbly again. As if the whole world out there is mine for the taking — when I know better.'

Matthews looked down at her. Some moments in life, no matter how inconsequential they seem at the time, are turning points for future and more important paths. In that single instant he sensed that simple attraction had seamlessly become love, for him.

'You should do that more often, Jo,' he said quietly.

'Do what?'

'Laugh. It's not just your face that changes . . . ' His voice tailed off.

'Go on,' she said. 'Don't stop there. I'm back to being young and silly again.'

Matthews gently turned her round and held her shoulders.

'You become a different person,' he said slowly. 'You become . . . '

He sensed her drawing in towards him, her face tilting up.

Gently at first, then with real passion, he kissed her. The dog leash fell to the floor as Jo returned his kiss. Then she pushed herself away from him.

'Oh dear,' she said breathlessly. 'Step four, sort of galloped in on us.'

Matthews picked up Ben's leash. The old dog was staring up at them, his tail slowly wagging. Whatever his humans were doing, it felt good. His canine senses almost saw the golden cloud of happiness which blossomed out from them.

There could be a biscuit in this for me, he thought.

* * *

It was mid-afternoon before Jo finished her dog-walking duties, and came with Matthews slowly down the woodland path towards the mill. As they reached the clearing on the far side of the stepping-stones she guiltily released his hand.

Not before Andy Morris had seen them from his vantage point on a ladder high against the side of the mill. Aye-aye, he thought. Then: good for Jo, it's time she had a bit of happiness. However, to save their blushes, he worked earnestly at the top window frame and professed surprise when they called up to him.

'Don't sneak up on me like that!' he exclaimed. 'I nearly fell off my ladder.'

'Sorry,' said Matthews. 'How's the work getting on?'

'We're getting there.' Andy descended.

'We're inside budget, that's the main thing This old mill was built to last, and there's been nothing major.' On reaching ground he shook Matthews's hand. 'Good to see you. There's something we need to talk about in the next phase of work — before we put it to Meg.'

'Go on,' said Matthews, his eyes on Jo as she pushed through into the mill.

Andy hid a grin. Nice guy: Jo would do well if she could land him.

'I've been thinking about what we might do with the top floor. Almost half the area is taken up with the millstones' machinery, and the rest is a big rambling bedroom. We could maybe restructure that, and plumb in a more modern toilet — with a shower and all the fancy trimmings.'

'If we're changing structure, we need to check out the conservation issues.'

'That's why I'm raising it with you,' Andy said. 'Meg has her hands full just now.'

'What do you mean?' asked Matthews, puzzled.

'Of course, you haven't seen her yet. Sorry. Well, we've spent the last two days getting the old bakery working again. It started as a plan to find a bigger oven for Jo's baking. Then Meg realized she had enough oven-space to bake bread as well. She's having a go at that tonight. I've got a grand old baker who has come over to teach her how . . . ' Andy broke off, seeing Matthews's face.

'It's all right,' he said testily. 'No extra charge. She helped me out, so I've taken a couple of days to help her too. That's how we do things up here.'

Matthews waved a placating hand. 'No, it's not that. You've caught me flat-footed; this is all news to me.'

Andy grinned. 'She's a rare one for taking the bit in her teeth and driving through changes. Single-minded, once she gets going. It started as curiosity — what sort of shape were the ovens in? Then came the idea that maybe she could help Jo. Then that she could maybe help herself as well, and build a small bakery business out of it. Once she gets going it's like the tide coming in.'

Matthews frowned. 'And is it workable? This bakery idea?'

Andy shrugged. 'Who knows? The ovens are in fine fettle, she's a quick learner, and Fred can teach her to bake decent bread for the markets. The point is . . . are these local markets enough to support a business? Both you and her bank manager would want to see the forecasts first. I'm an engineer. All I was interested in was could I make the system work again?'

171

Matthews rubbed his neck. 'Our original intentions are growing arms and legs. Where would this leave us with your conservation people?'

'I'm not sure — that's why I wanted to speak to you. Up to now we're OK; we've been repairing and restoring damage caused by dereliction, using traditional methods and materials. That usually goes past on the nod, in my experience of listed buildings. But modern loos are different — they're at least a planning issue, with the conservation view taken on board. And does a new bakery business count as restarting one that ran maybe sixty years ago?'

Andy grimaced. 'I think we're already into conservation territory, and they will hammer us if we change things first, then ask for permission second. It's the letting sleeping dogs lie problem: when do you wake them up, and how? My advice is to bring in an outside specialist to discuss what's possible and what isn't. I know a good young local architect who does listed buildings and often helps out the conservation people. He could advise us, then maybe negotiate a deal with them, if Meg decides to go ahead.'

'Have you talked about this to her yet?'

'She's been too busy — the bakery idea is taking up every minute.'

Matthews struggled to bring his mind back to business mode. 'It's silly to take unnecessary risks,' he muttered. 'Let's meet your architect, get him to run an eye over everything — what we've done, what Meg might want to do. Establish the facts, before we bite off more than we can chew.'

The two men pushed through the mill door, to find Meg and Jo deep in a working tutorial. Meg was up to her elbows in flour, kneading dough on the freshly scrubbed old bakery table.

'Why shouldn't it work?' Fred was demanding. 'If we can produce a loaf that tastes lik' bread an' not polystyrene, it'll sell in shops as well as t' market.'

'I'm not even sure Phil would want bread for the market,' Jo said, frowning.

'Nay! Keep that dough working, lass!' Fred snapped at Meg. 'Give Phil a slice o' buttered fresh bread, an' one bite will convince him. It's mass production agin' proper craftsman skill. The more time an' effort put into bakin' bread, the more it pays you back in t' flavour. Nay, lass! Tha needs t'work dough harder — slap it about a bit! Here, let me show thee.'

He stripped off his old jacket and took the big roll of dough from her.

'Like this,' he said, lifting it up and pounding it down on the table, then repeatedly thrusting his fists hard and deep into it. 'Treat it like tha hates it . . . tek anger out on't. Work it hard. The more muscle tha puts int' it, the more air's in t' dough, an' the better it rises, an' the better it fires.'

He worked busily for a few minutes, the tendons standing out starkly on his scrawny wrists, but the fists below them were big and competent and doing the job they'd always done. Bakers develop the hand-power of a blacksmith.

'That's better,' he said. 'Tekk over and finish 't off.'

He turned back to Andy, eyes twinkling.

'It's lik' fallin' off bike,' he said. 'Tha nivver forgets how.' Then he nodded at Jo. 'Now you get goin',' he ordered.

'I've only a few minutes . . . '

'Then use 'em proper. Get kneading on t' next batch. That's better, lass,' he said, watching Meg again. 'That's got t' hands.'

'But not the brain,' puffed Meg.

'Who needs brain?' Fred demanded. 'Brain only gets thee int' trouble. It's hands that count. Now cut dough into loaves, for tray.'

He watched, nodding, as Meg cut off the dough into the lumps which would rise into loaves. 'That's it,' he said. 'Now for t' secret ingredient. The invisible secret that modern bakeries have all lost.'

'What's that?' asked Meg, resting on floury hands.

'Time,' said Fred. 'Nowadays it's continuous-process baking. Dough is pounded, cut, then stuck straight int' oven. Boss would have had me shot for that, as apprentice.'

He looked around, checking the effect of his words. 'Whole secret of good bread is in leaving dough to prove,' he declared. 'What you bake tomorrow morning, you make this afternoon. Then leave it. That lets the yeast grow natural. That's how we did it in my day. An' the bread we baked hurt nobody — not like now.'

'That's old grannies' tales!' Jo protested.

'It's as true as I'm sitting here. Leave yeast to prove overnight, an' your bread will trouble nobody.'

He glanced at Robert. 'Is this another learner?' he demanded. 'There's room on t' table yet.'

'Don't let him near your dough,' panted Jo. 'He's a better lawyer than he is a baker. Trust me. He ruined two batches of scones for me last night.'

'Takes all kinds,' sighed Fred.

'Horses for courses,' Matthews agreed.

'An' no point in teaching Andy. He can't even mix cement.'

'My cement looks better than your dough.'

'Cheeky beggar!' said Fred. 'Come on, then. What's tha all stoppin' for, an' listenin'? We have bread t' mek.'

'Told you he was a tyrant,' observed Andy. 'I reckon he were foreman, when Egyptians put up t' pyramids. He's old enough for that.'

'I've lasted longer than some o' them pyramids,' said Fred. 'They mun have got t'mixture wrong.'

*　*　*

After the others had gone Matthews searched for Meg and found her sitting on the big rock beside the stepping-stones. She was flipping pebbles into the shallow water of the ford, and frowning.

'Penny for your thoughts,' he said, sitting down beside her.

Meg glanced up, startled. 'They're not worth a penny,' she said.

'Give you a ha'penny then.'

'Are they still legal currency?'

'What's worrying you?' he asked directly.

'Everything.' She gave a sigh. 'For a start, I seem to be spending money like water. I'm scared of what you're going to say to me about that.'

'That's easy,' said Matthews. 'It's your money, and therefore yours to spend. If I thought you were throwing it away on fripperies, then I would slam the brake on at some point soon. But once we accept your quirky decision to live in this old mill, all the money spent has had a sober purpose. And, having seen the mill on an evening like this, I can fully understand why you want to live here — so even that first decision stops being quirky.'

'That's one worry less.' Meg sounded relieved. 'I've spent more in the last few days, than in the last twenty years. It's really spooking me.'

'Over those twenty years you didn't have money to spend. Now you do.'

'It still takes a bit of getting used to.' Meg flipped another stone. 'Then there's this bakery,' she added. 'I wanted to help Jo, but the idea ran away with me. Now I'm starting to worry that I'm doing it only for myself.'

Matthews leaned down, picked up a pebble and studied it.

'What's wrong with that?' he replied after a moment or two. 'You're relatively rich, but funds are finite. At some stage you'll have to look for another job. Sure, you could sell off your mill and go back to Edinburgh, and live for a bit on that new capital. But I think you'd prefer to stay here. If you can set up your own business by reopening the bakery, then you've made a niche for yourself in Kirkby. And if working here helps Jo to make ends meet, then you have been a true friend and helped her too.'

'I want to make her a partner.'

'Too soon to think of that.'

'Will the bakery work?' Meg asked.

'Too many questions still to answer. Can these old ovens produce bread and cakes which will sell? If they do, can you sell enough to support a business? If you can . . . will the local conservation people let you reopen the bakery as well as rescue the building itself?'

'I hadn't thought of that,' Meg muttered.

'Andy did. We were discussing it earlier. We'd like you to bring in an architect who works on listed buildings, to take his advice.'

Meg smiled slowly. 'Good old Andy, always one step ahead of me.'

'Not necessarily. More experienced in building repairs, therefore more aware of the potential problems.'

Meg flipped another stone into the river, watching its ripples widen through the gentle stream. 'Then there's me,' she said quietly. 'A few weeks ago I was a loner, having talked myself out of a job. No friends worth speaking of — they all melted away while I was looking for work, in case they caught the same disease.' She smiled grimly. 'Nothing like sickness or unemployment to sift out your friends.'

'And . . . ?' Matthews prompted.

Meg coloured. 'And I have found a friend in Jo, who will back me to the hilt when it really matters. In pails and mops, if that's what it takes, not empty words and promises.' She glanced at Matthews. 'And in a lawyer whom I once thought was terrifying, I've found a friend whom I can talk to, and whose opinions and advice I really heed. For which, thanks, Robert.'

'Friendship works two ways,' he said mildly.

'I know. But I have found . . . almost a father figure. I feel secure, when I know you're looking after what I'm doing.'

Suddenly, she couldn't bring herself to go on.

'Then there's Andy,' Matthews gently prompted.

'Yes,' she said. 'There's Andy. I'm getting all the boundaries confused — and I'm not sure which way to turn.'

'Join the club,' he said.

Meg flashed a look at him. 'You, and Jo?'

He nodded. 'No fool like an old fool. Only I'm anything but a fool. Maybe, just maybe, I'm the luckiest guy on earth.'

'Jo's the most good-hearted person I've met,' said Meg. 'I'm happy for her, if things work out — happy for you too.'

'But?' prompted Matthews.

Meg threw her last stone into the river. 'But I just wish I was as certain about myself. What I'm doing . . . letting happen, what I'm feeling. Am I so vulnerable that I'm starting to fall for a local builder, who has done nothing more than be nice to me? Even if I know he's not just a hunk, but a bright and educated man who has chosen to step out of the rat race and work like his father did. It's years since I met anyone I liked so much, had so much in common with. Am I simply overreacting to somebody decent? This is ridiculous! To be talking like this, to my lawyer — and not to another woman friend.'

Matthews smiled. 'Hey, lassie!' he rebuked her gently. 'You're allowed men friends as well. Even if one of them is a lawyer.'

'I'm not sure what to do,' she whispered.

'Are you happy, as things stand now?' he asked.

She flashed another look at him. 'I've never been so happy.'

'Me neither.' He sighed. 'So I guess the same advice applies to both of us.'

'Which is?'

'*Carpe diem*,' Matthews said. 'An old Latin

saying. *Seize the day*. Enjoy it for what it offers, because it will never come again, and nobody knows what the future will bring. Don't be afraid of the present. Don't shirk from accepting what it gives. Then, whatever worries and problems come tomorrow, you haven't wasted the gift of today.'

Meg sniffed. 'You've done it again,' she said.

'Done what?'

'Stepped in and been a father figure, shown me the way forward.'

Matthews grimaced. 'Rubbish!' he said. 'I was advising myself.' He looked down at the stone in his hand. 'Here. You've already used up the rest of the beach. There's no point in keeping this one.' He stood up. 'Well, I'm off.'

'Going to Fadmoor?' she asked.

He nodded.

'Good luck!' she called after him, as he stepped easily across the river.

⋆   ⋆   ⋆

There was barely any light in the sky when Meg's alarm went off. Sleepily she reached out an arm, knocking the clock off the edge of the sofa. Outside, even the birds were silent. She lay woozily, listening to the liquid murmur of the river across the ford, and the sigh of the wind through the trees.

Reality forced itself into her mind. Sitting up, she kicked off the covers.

Today had been planned with the precision of a military attack. No time in that for any dreaming. She washed in cold water, yelping as it stung her skin. The sooner she had electricity connected again, the better. Living rough as if camping was fine — but not at 5.30 in the morning.

She bolted enough of a breakfast to keep herself going, and poured some black coffee from a thermos she had filled in the hotel the night before. Mug in hand, she skimmed down the stairs in the half-light, and looked apprehensively at the silent bakery waiting for her below.

Once before there had been a match, a friend, and good wishes. Now she was on her own. Taking a gulp of coffee, which scorched her throat, she fumbled for a match and lit two of the oil lamps. They would give her light until the dawn came. She got down in her knees, and opened the door to the firebox.

Everything was as she had left it, waiting only for a match. As she went to strike it, there came a knock at the door.

'Come in!' she called, sitting back on her heels.

The door opened on two dim figures. One tall and broad-shouldered. The other smaller, stockier, but hammered into soundest steel on the forge of life.

'Andy . . . Jo . . . ' she said, her eyes filling.

'Can't have you mucking up the bread on your own,' said Jo. 'Give me those matches, before you burn yourself.'

She stooped down, taking the box from Meg's slack fingers.

'I spoke to Phil, from the market, last night. He said if he likes the look and taste of it, he'll run our bread in his stall today. Purely as an experiment, no final judgement or commitment on either side. And I forced him to double what he was offering us for a dozen loaves. Six dozen, he wants to start with. The market is over in Helmsley today. So we have to get them there for seven thirty.'

On her knees before the fire, she looked up. 'Robert's driving us over,' she said. 'He wanted to be here with me and Andy, but I told him he'd be useless until the bread was done. I said to wait and get some breakfast at the hotel — they'll charge him for it anyway, whether he eats it or not.'

She sparked the match. 'So it's all systems go,' she said, reaching in and applying the flame to the tails of rolled-up paper. She watched as the fire caught, then closed the metal door. 'That's us. I brought coffee for us to drink, while we're waiting for the ovens to heat up.'

Meg shook her head, too full of gratitude to speak. Her friends were here, as good friends should be. Unbidden, when they were needed.

'And you?' she said unsteadily to Andy. 'Why are you here?'

'Somebody has to spit int' oven,' he said. 'Then listen to the sizzle.'

It started as a laugh, then somehow became a flood of tears. Meg found herself wrapped round Andy's chest, sobbing her heart out. Felt him pat her back gently, then smooth her hair. His lips silently brushed her head.

'Go on,' said Jo from the floor. 'Give the woman a decent hug. She won't break in two.'

8

'I think your guy's asking us over, Jo,' Meg muttered.

At the far side of the market square, the stall-holder's hand beckoned to them again. The two women had come back to check out how their bread was selling, and were watching nervously from a safe distance, as locals and visitors thronged the street market.

'We'd better see what he wants,' said Jo.

'He looks pretty grim. What if the bread's a disaster?' Meg asked, her heart in her mouth.

'Grim? That's a Yorkshireman's smile!' Jo scoffed. 'The bread's good, and Phil's a decent guy. Come on, we've nothing to worry about.' Impatiently, Jo took Meg's arm and steered her through the Helmsley shoppers.

Phil was wrapping one of Jo's large cakes for a customer as they reached him. 'Half the price of t'local bakery's cakes, an' twice as good,' he assured the woman, then turned to Jo.

'Well?' she demanded.

'Where's the two guys who were with you this morning?'

'Gone back to work,' said Jo. 'How's the bread selling?'

Phil nodded. 'It's doing away reet nicely,' he admitted, as if the confession was forced from him. 'There's only about two dozen left in t' van. Promising, very promising. The real test will be if they ask for more next Friday.' He glanced at Meg. 'I'm taking a punt on you, missus. I think we might have a modest goer in that bread. Market's at Malton tomorrow, with the big Saturday crowd. Can you do me ten dozen? Turn me int' proper baker's shop.' A sudden white grin split his sombre face.

'Of course we can,' said Jo.

'It were her I was speakin' to,' Phil nodded towards Meg.

'And it was me that answered. We can do ten dozen.'

Phil frowned. 'Mind you, bit of a gamble, this. I'm looking for a better discount — seein' as I'm buying almost double.'

'On your bike!' snorted Jo.

'Your friend's doin' a grand ventriloquist act,' Phil said admiringly. 'Haven't seen her lips move once.'

'We're in this together,' said Jo. 'And I know you're a chancer — can't help yourself — while Meg might give you the benefit of the doubt.'

'That's slander, she's talkin',' Phil protested to Meg.

Meg smiled. 'Only if it's not the truth,' she replied. 'And I somehow think it is. We can do your ten dozen — it's a gamble for us too. Same price, same time tomorrow. Deal.'

'See,' said Jo. 'She can talk for herself.'

Phil sighed. 'What chance have I, against two hard-hearted Scotswomen?' he mourned. 'I'm just a poor struggling street trader.'

'Stop,' mocked Jo. 'You'll ha'e me greetin'.'

The same white smile flashed again. 'So long as tears don't spoil the dough,' Phil said.

'They improve the flavour,' said Meg. 'Add that extra dash of salt.'

'Tomorrow, then,' said Phil. He turned to a new customer. 'What can I do for you?' he asked. 'Better cakes, at half the price of baker's shop. And a special deal on new line we are running . . . bread like it used to taste when we were young — that's fifteen years ago for you, m' dear.'

Over the elderly woman's head, one eye winked at them.

'I don't know how he ever sells,' sighed Jo. 'He cheeks-up everybody.'

They walked slowly back to the car parked a couple of streets away from the market. All at once, Meg's legs felt leaden, moving them took all the strength she had. She started to speak, then a yawn took over — a huge yawn that made her fear her jaw might crack and jam on her.

Jo smiled. 'Tired?' she asked. 'That's the early start.'

'More likely the tension,' Meg replied. 'I feel shattered.'

'You've launched our new bread line. A good morning's work.'

'But will it really succeed — or is this just a one-off novelty?'

'That Phil has never lost a penny on a deal. He could buy and sell both of us, and have cash to spare. He knows his market. He ate three slices of bread and butter, before he set up his stall. Then I saw him put away a couple of loaves, and some teabread — that was for himself. Trust me. He knows a winner.'

They opened Jo's car and flopped wearily into it.

'Where now?' asked Jo. 'I have dogs to walk.'

'The mill,' said Meg. 'Drop me off in Kirkby, and I'll hike home.'

'My first dog's Ben,' said Jo. 'I'll bring him too.'

* * *

Meg stepped across the river's stones, a brisk breeze sending her hair flying round her face. Halfway across she stopped, looked up. Her heart lifted to see the huge square shape of the sandstone mill and, in fanciful mood, she sensed that its heart lifted too. She loved this place, and how it had changed her life.

How Henry Waterston had changed her life, she corrected herself. She had been so preoccupied with settling in, then starting up the bakery again, that the memory of her unknown uncle and benefactor had been pushed away.

'Thank you, Henry,' she whispered, as the river gurgled round her.

Her eye was drawn to the collection of cars outside the mill: Andy's pick-up, her own car, Robert's small hire car — and a large shining black Range Rover. Her tired mind stuttered, then she realized this must be the architect that Andy and Robert were bringing out to advise on the conservation issues. Tucking her hair back, she hurried across the remaining stones.

Entering into the bakery took her back into the wonderful smell of freshly baked bread. Her stomach rumbled. When had she last eaten? Upstairs, she heard the rumble of men's voices. Taking a deep breath, she went nimbly up the open stairs into her living space, then up the next flight into the loft and its ancient bedroom.

The men were studying the rusted and silent mill machinery; they turned as her footsteps sounded behind them.

'Well, how's the market going?' asked Robert.

'Promising. Phil wants us to do ten dozen loaves for tomorrow.'

'That's good,' said Robert. 'This is Paul. Paul Chesney, the architect.'

Meg nodded. 'Have Andy and Robert shown you around?' she asked.

'He's torn half the mill apart,' complained Andy. 'Now I've got to stick it back together again.'

Chesney smiled at the alarm on Meg's face. 'Not quite,' he said. 'But yes, the three of us have had a long and thorough look at the fabric of the place — Andy's been really helpful.'

'He even made us a cup of tea,' Robert said.

'I hope he washed up afterwards,' replied Meg.

'Nay, lass,' said Andy, mournfully. 'Clearin' up 'tis women's work.'

'He's been busy,' said Chesney. 'I've kept them both on the hop.'

'It's the only way to treat them,' agreed

Meg. 'How do we stand? In terms of the conservation regulations?'

The architect stroked his chin. 'I'd like to run it past the local conservation people, but my gut hunch is that you're OK — Andy has seen to that. The repair work he's done has kept the original fabric wherever possible, like replacing window sections rather than entire frames. And the glass which he's used is old glass — absolutely essential, that.'

Andy grinned at Meg's blank face. 'Old glass is rough and bubbly,' he explained. 'It's uneven surface makes it sparkle in the sun. Modern glass is absolutely flat — and thicker, too. It doesn't sparkle. I always buy up old glass when I see it. Then keep it for old houses, when we're doing replacements.'

'Oh,' said Meg, only a little wiser.

'Andy has also used traditional repair methods and material,' Chesney continued. 'Linseed oil putty, sand-based mastic, old-style mortar. Again essential, in conservation work. So if this is a listed building, we can put through everything that he's done as 'necessary repairs and maintenance'. That normally gets passed on the nod, with a simple exchange of letters or emails, because you haven't changed the appearance or the nature of the building.'

'But *are* we a listed building?' asked Meg.

'That's the first thing to check,' agreed Chesney. 'The local authority should have a record of all listed buildings in its area. If not, then English Heritage hold the master lists. A few minutes work with records will sort that out. I'm guessing you're a Grade 2 — that means of local architectural and historical interest, and therefore important to maintain, but not of major national heritage significance. Be grateful — that's fewer hoops to jump through.'

'What about us reopening the bakery?' Meg asked.

'Tricky, but my gut hunch is that we can probably argue it through on the same 'repair and maintenance' basis — claiming that all we've done is to restore the ovens into full running order, as part of our strategy for returning the mill building to its original condition. Provided we can prove that this once functioned as a bakery.'

'Then we're OK?' Meg said, with relief.

Chesney shot a look at Matthews. 'Yes and no,' he said. 'We may have to do a bit of horse-trading with the conservators.'

'For the new toilet?' Meg asked, puzzled.

'Absolutely not. That's a structural change — you will need to apply to planning, with all the usual drawings of floor and elevations. Again there's a goodish prognosis, because you're not changing the appearance of the building. No, we were discussing something different . . . a real bargaining weapon that should get the conservators on our side, supporting our case for all the changes.'

'What Paul has suggested,' Andy chipped in, thinking that Chesney was taking for ever, 'is that you should think about bringing the millstones back into operation, at the end of the reconstruction work.'

'But why?' Meg asked.

'Any conservator will jump at the chance to fully restore a working mill,' Chesney explained. 'They will bend over backwards to help you with grants and loans to finance the rebuilding.' He shrugged. 'It's politics, of course, but it makes sense to use leverage as and where you find it.'

'What benefit would I get from having the millstones working again?' Meg demanded.

'You can demonstrate that you have brought the whole process in-house,' Chesney replied. 'Grinding your own flour, then using it in the bakery. The original economic purpose, as well as the mill building itself, has been restored.'

Neither Robert nor Andy met her eye.

'We need time to discuss this,' she said. 'Too much information, too quickly. I'd like to think this through with Robert and Andy.'

'Of course,' Chesney said. 'Wouldn't want anything else. In the meantime, I will check out your listed status . . . and maybe test the water about the rest.'

'Robert?' Meg addressed him directly.

He shrugged. 'This whole project keeps growing. My priority today was to take advice on whether or not we had overstepped the mark in our conversion work, particularly in reopening the old bakery. I knew that any changes to the structure — like the bedroom — would need planning permission. Reactivating the millwheels never crossed my mind. I can see the conservation value — but my job is to protect your personal interests. That, I really need to think about.'

'That goes for me too,' said Andy.

'OK,' Meg said crisply. 'Then we need time to consider before we come to a decision.'

'Agreed,' said Chesney. 'While I explore the options open to you.'

*　　*　　*

Meg felt exhausted, but her mind wouldn't settle and she had the dough to prepare for baking ten dozen loaves the following morning. She made a couple of mugs of tea, and took one out to Andy — perched high on his ladders and working above. He came slowly down and took the tea from her without comment.

They walked down to the rock at the river's edge and sat there, noticeably apart. For once, there was no easy sense of friendship between them. Not good, she thought; only a few hours before she had been in this man's arms, had felt his lips brush across her hair.

'Where do we go from here, Andy?' she asked quietly.

'With the millwheels?' he answered, staring over the river.

'No, with us.'

He shot her a look; for once the humour was absent in his eyes.

'Maybe I overstepped myself?' he said at last. 'Maybe I just wanted to help — and you were stressed out, not your usual self? Maybe things just happened, accidental like, and we should make darn sure we don't go there again.'

'Is that what you really think?' she asked, pain in her voice.

Her heart counted the seconds while she waited for an answer.

Then his head came up, eyes steady. 'No,' he said simply.

Meg's heart lifted. 'It's not what I think, either.'

'Boy meets girl. Boy likes girl. Hey, but we're mekkin' a right old meal o'this.'

Meg smiled. 'Absolutely. It's caught us both out a bit.'

'That's for sure.' His words were heartfelt.

The river gurgled past them in the silence of the glade. Andy picked up a pebble that had survived Meg's earlier attempt to clear the beach. He flipped it easily into the pool above the stepping-stones, and watched the ripples spread.

'Happen I do have a strong opinion about the millstones,' he said quietly.

'Then out with it,' she replied, setting the empty mug at her feet.

'I think it's wrong for you — to go ahead and reconstruct the mill.'

'Why?'

He grimaced. 'If what you're doing in life is small, then you're in full control of both it and your life. Like the bakery here. You can keep it as a lifestyle business, earning enough to make ends meet and leaving yourself with plenty of time to enjoy your life and your friends and the place about you. But the bigger it grows, the grander the plan, the weaker is your control. First, you're hanging on by your fingertips; then, one day, your fingers slip, then your business runs away with you. You become its slave, and it sucks up all your choices, your time, your energy . . . until finally there's nothing left to give it but your life.'

A silence, broken by the river running through the stones.

'Is that why you came back to your dad's business?' Meg asked at last.

'It is,' he answered. 'I got tired of jetting round the world and waking up in strange hotels. My phone never stopping ringing, and my email bulging with questions and demands from people I'd never meet yet who worked in the same organization as myself. I got tired of finding corruption everywhere — it's a whole different culture out there. Nothing gets done without a bribe, or a favour, or a piece of inside knowledge changing hands. You get to feel so tired, so dirty . . . so utterly lost. Then you realize that you're betraying all the decent principles your dad crammed into you as a child. That's it — the point where you either hand over your life completely, or come out and look for something different, where you can find yourself again. Turn the clock back to when life was simpler — and more honest. That's why I came home. I'm glad Dad lived to see me taking over his tools.'

'Bravo!' she said quietly.

He rose, his eyes on the tree tops across the river, watching them dance in the brisk Yorkshire breeze. 'Success is hollow. I'd hate to watch anyone making the same mistakes as

I did, least of all, you.' His eyes came back to hold hers steadily. 'You have a new home, you have a new business, you are happy — I can read all that in your face. Settle for what you've got, Meg.'

He reached down, took her hand and lifted her effortlessly to her feet.

'Where we go from here, the two of us, I don't quite know,' he said. 'It feels right, and that's as far as I've considered it. You are everything I've ever wanted in a woman, Meg. But right now, you are vulnerable, making a new start everywhere. You're too dependent. It's not the time for either of us to rush into something that could spoil, or destroy, what we've only just found.'

The serious face softened, and the twinkle came back into his eyes.

'Eee, lass,' he said. 'If tha wants me t' say that I'm sorry for kissin' thee, then I'm not.'

Meg squeezed the big rough hand which held her own.

'Me neither,' she said. 'Let's go. We both have work to do.'

*   *   *

The tiny stream ran through ferns and tinkled over a six-inch waterfall. Matthews sat, as still as he could manage, his back aching from the

198

weight which lay heavily against his shoulder. Jo's hair tickled his face. He let it itch, stopping the rising hand which had been going to brush it away.

Down at his feet the ancient Labrador snored loudly, and wakened himself up. He woke Jo too. She gave a startled exclamation, struggling to gather her senses from the deep sleep which had scattered them.

'I must have fallen asleep,' she said, shamefaced.

'Only a few minutes,' said Matthews. 'You were tired. You do too much.'

'I'm used to it.' Her head still felt muzzy. 'Was that me who snored?'

'No. Ben.'

'Are you sure? You're not trying to save my feelings.'

'Cross my heart,' he said with a grin. 'Until a couple of weeks ago I didn't know I had one.'

'What time is it?' Jo asked. She glanced at her watch. 'You liar, Robert — I've been sleeping for nearly an hour.' She rose stiffly. 'Let's take Ben back — because I still have one more dog to walk. I'm so sorry. I've never fallen asleep like that before.'

Because she'd never felt so secure, so content, for many years, she realized. Relaxed, trusting, able to lower all defences with this man. She was afraid even to put her thoughts into words. She was either a trollop — or the luckiest woman on earth. To have found such a love and such happiness again . . . in another man who was different in every way from Jim.

'Come on, Robert,' she said. 'We have to hurry — or I'll be late again in picking up the kids from school.'

'I'll collect them for you,' he offered.

'Is that wise? There's no problem with Anna — she's your fan. Even if we take away all the help you give her in her homework, she still likes you. But Jamie . . . he's such a grump. So impossible and rude.'

'With good reason. He sees me coming in to throw out his father's memory and steal his mum. He doesn't know what to think — that makes him defensive.'

'But you wouldn't throw out Jim's memory!'

'Of course not. But that's why he's so suspicious of me.'

'Suspicious? He acts as if he hates you!'

'He probably does.' Matthews sighed. 'So it's up to me to try and find a way to reach him, get him to talk about it. To understand that the past can never be obliterated by anyone . . . but to accept that there is a future too. And I'm not going to build that bridge by keeping out of his way, or sheltering behind your skirts. It has to be *mano a mano* — only in the sense of mind to mind, rather than hand to hand.'

'Is that more Latin?' Jo asked resignedly.

Matthew grinned: as always it took years from his face. 'No, Spanish, I think. It comes from the old bull-fighting days, when the toreador took on the bull by hand and courage alone.'

'Is there anything you don't know?' Jo smiled.

'Lots. Like whether or not you would like to bring the kids to the hotel, for a meal tonight?'

'So, my cooking isn't good enough for you?'

'Of course it is. But you're tired — and there are still scones to bake at Meg's tonight.'

'And bread . . . I think we've struck gold in these ovens. Meg wants me to give up this dog-walking. Then split with her what we earn from the old bakery.'

They walked down from the moor, holding hands.

'You have still to make that work,' Matthews warned.

'Oh, we will,' said Jo. 'It *has* to work. There's so much depending on it, for both of us.'

'Then count me in.'

'No chance!' exclaimed Jo. 'We need to make bread that sells.'

'Then let me be your legal adviser,' teased Matthews.

'That depends on your charges,' warned Jo, her face alive with amusement.

'One kiss, before and after. Then at my side, for evermore.'

Jo stopped in her tracks. 'Do you realize what you've just said?'

'Yes.'

'So what's this 'before and after'?'

'Before and after finding a way to bring Jamie on board.'

The light slowly died in Jo's face.

'Hell might freeze over first,' she said.

* * *

'Problems?' Meg asked.

Matthews grimaced. 'Is it that obvious?'

'You look down.'

'Not down. Challenged.'

'Jo?'

'Absolutely not.' Matthews was unusually clipped.

'The boy?'

Matthews nodded. 'Another meal, another disaster, last night. When are you getting hooked up to mains electricity again?'

He didn't want to talk about the problem, Meg realized.

'Tomorrow, Andy says,' she replied. 'I'm looking forward to that. It will be nice to have hot water again, and to be able to cook a proper meal.'

Matthews gave a wry grimace. 'I suppose it's the price you have had to pay for moving in, before the mill was fully ready to be lived in.'

'Worth it,' she said stoutly. 'I love living here.'

He watched her potter round the old kitchen, tidying away breakfast dishes which had been washed in water boiled on Andy's primus stove. The young are adaptable, he thought; born to survive whatever life throws at them.

'Maybe I should have argued more strongly against you settling in so quickly?' he teased.

'I wouldn't have listened. I love the privacy of this place, the sound of the river running past, of the wind brushing through the trees. The whole sense of peace. And nowhere do I feel that more strongly than up in the old bedroom, which Andy has still to rescue. I love sitting on the window seat and looking out.'

'Don't you ever feel lonely? Scared?'

'That's the strange thing . . . I'm never really alone in here. It always feels as if somebody is sitting in the old armchair, both watching me and watching over me — like a wise old grandmother, nodding her approval.'

Matthews winced. 'That would send me fleeing from the place.'

'Not at all. It feels . . . reassuring. Invisible, but kind. Benign. I keep snatching a glance across, hoping to catch a glimpse of something. I often wonder exactly who is keeping me company.'

'Henry Waterston?' asked Matthews, remembering the man's face, full of love as he sat in the lawyer's office and dictated the terms of his will, leaving Meg the sole beneficiary.

Meg frowned. 'I've often wondered,' she said. 'But it doesn't feel like a man, somehow — too gentle.' She put away the last plate and wiped down the kitchen surfaces. 'I'm glad you mentioned him. Now that I've settled into his mill — '

'Your mill.'

She nodded. 'Now that I've settled in, I would like to find out more about Henry — the mystery uncle I never knew existed. Just a little about his background, so that I can start to understand why he came from nowhere to leave me such a wonderful gift.' She glanced up. 'Robert, what do you know about Henry Waterston?'

'Not much.' Matthews struggled to recall what was in his office files in London. 'We had the address of his flat, of course, but he wasn't a client who had regular dealings with us. Indeed, I don't remember any business apart from his will. Perhaps there was something in my father's time . . . '

'Are there any other members of my family I should know about?'

'Pass. To find that out would take a census records search. There are specialist researchers you could commission, to chase down your family roots. But, from what I've heard, it's much more fun to chase them down yourself.'

'No time for that,' Meg said. 'I have a business to set on its feet.'

Matthews pushed himself away from the doorframe. 'I can phone Alison, my secretary, and ask her to run a quick check over what's in our files — but I doubt there will be much on offer there.'

'Please. If it's not too much trouble. It's just . . . I feel it's the very least I can do for Henry, by way of saying 'thanks' posthumously. Try to find out more about the man, touch his roots. Then maybe lay some flowers on his grave.'

'We can tell you where that is.'

'Too soon. I want to find out what sort of man he was, why he became a fairy godfather and completely changed my life, so that I can

stand beside his grave and feel real kinship
— as well as gratitude — before I close the
circle.'

From outside came the crunching of tyres
on the gravel track.

'That will be Andy,' Meg said eagerly.

'Chesney too. There's his four-by-four.'

Meg craned, looking through the kitchen
windows. 'Have you had time to consider
what Chesney suggested?'

'Not really,' Matthews replied. 'My main
concern is to anchor down that what we are
doing here — both in repairs and starting up
the old bakery again — conforms to the law.
I'm not really sure that we should be thinking
too far ahead of that, as yet. Better learning to
walk, before we try to run.'

'That's more or less what Andy says.'

Meg skimmed downstairs and opened the
door. She smiled up at Andy. 'I suppose I had
better get the primus lit again?'

'If you insist,' said Andy. He stepped inside
the door and waved Chesney through. 'Maybe
it's champagne you should be opening,' he
added.

'Good news?' asked Matthews.

'Better than I hoped,' said the architect.
'But I'll have tea, if that's what everybody else
is drinking.'

'Come upstairs and tell us your news while

the kettle's boiling,' Meg said.

'I'll make the tea,' offered Andy. 'I've heard his story already.'

Meg ushered them up into her living area. 'Well?' she demanded.

'Firstly,' said Chesney, 'my guess was right. The mill is a Grade 2 listed building, therefore we need the conservation officer's blessing on anything we do to it.' He ran fingers through his hair. 'I described the work already carried out, and the traditional methods used. No problems. All she needs is a letter detailing this, and she will send back her approval. She may come out to check, but that should be a formality.'

'The bakery?' Matthews asked.

'She's actually very keen on that, and sees it as an important element of your conservation project.'

'That's a relief,' said Matthews. 'The redesign of the big bedroom and toilet?'

'A standard planning application — forms, plans, the usual. Again it will also need the conservation officer's approval to go through, so she will be coming out to check that any changes don't radically alter the appearance or nature of the building. Thanks . . . ' he accepted a mug from the tray Andy carried in.

'I'm getting too domesticated,' Andy

complained. 'She'll have me tying on an apron next. Have you got to the best bit yet?'

'Just reaching it.' Chesney sipped from his mug. 'When I told her about the millwheels machinery and the sluice, that absolutely made her morning. She jumped from her chair and started pacing the office. A fully working, locally historic mill in an area which is already popular with tourists! She says if we can get the mill to grind corn again she will personally steer you through the application, and help you with negotiating grants and loans. Plus she will get the tourism people on-side — she said they will jump at the chance to have a fully operational mill, grinding its own flour and making its own bread. Which means that all these officials will back you to the hilt — and with that level of support, you can't fail.'

'Oh dear,' said Meg. She glanced at Matthews.

He shrugged. 'Nothing is without cost,' he said. 'Sure, you will have strong financial support — but you will still have to find pound for pound of public money at the very least, from your own resources. While if you are opening up the mill to the public, the whole cost of reconstruction rises . . . you will need to install approved toilets, walkways, car parking, brochures. You are likely to triple, even quadruple, the reconstruction costs. I'd need to see the estimates, of course, but you don't have that sort of money left from Waterston's estate. You would have to sell your Edinburgh flat — and probably borrow too.'

'There would be soft loans available,' interjected Chesney. 'Easier to negotiate because of the authorities' support, and lower than commercial interest rates.'

Matthews frowned. 'It all sounds very tempting, but it still doesn't change my earlier advice. A full reconstruction programme doesn't need to be carried out now, it is something that could be considered later, years down the track.'

'I disagree,' said Chesney. 'The time to strike is while the iron's hot. If you act now, you have guaranteed support from the conservation office — the whole project will be a shoo-in. If you refuse to consider opening up the millwheels again, you could have one very annoyed officer, who has still to give her approval to everything else you're doing. That's the very real risk of doing nothing.'

Meg winced. Why did the world always want to complicate things?

'Andy, what do you think? What's your advice?' she asked.

'In engineering terms, it is challenging, but there is no reason why we shouldn't be able to fully restore the mill. In personal terms, like Robert, my earlier advice hasn't changed. Stay small . . . stay in full control of your life. But . . . '

'But what?'

'It's your life,' he said quietly. 'And you're the only one who can live it. So all the advice in the world doesn't matter. It has to be your choice — not ours.'

9

Amazing how quickly you dropped into the routine, Meg thought. Dough preparation — often still under Fred's eagle eye — in mid afternoon, while Jo was picking up her kids from school. Then helping Jo out in the evenings, baking cakes and teabread in the oven. Then up before the birds to fire the oven, bringing it up to temperature, and baking the trays of loaves. In time for Jo to drop in with her old estate car, and take as much as she could carry to the market, Meg following with the back seats of her smaller car flat and the whole rear stacked to the ceiling with bread.

'We'll need to get a small van,' she muttered to Jo. 'If we're going to do this as professionals, we need to think like professionals.'

'Not yet,' said Jo. 'Let's wait until we're sure, and not risk throwing good money away.'

Her sturdy commonsense was worth its weight in business experience: and although working even more hours out of twenty-four, she refused to give up her dog-walking, and somehow fitted that in too.

'It's crazy,' Meg said. 'We're earning more now than you ever did before.'

'Yes,' Jo replied. 'I know. But let's be absolutely sure, before I give up clients it has taken me years to win.'

Under this pressure of work, it was hard to think further ahead than the immediate task. Robert was right: even learning to walk took time and trying to run was quite impossible. The long-term nature of the reconstruction of the mill was put on to a back burner by default — Meg was simply too busy. When the conservation officer made an appointment to come and chat through the position in a fortnight's time, Meg accepted gladly.

Two weeks ahead was in a different life.

Robert watched with an approving eye. He went south to London once, for a few days, then returned, saying there were more important things going on in Kirkby than down in London. Meg felt sorry for him; Jamie was proving a hard nut to crack.

Andy completed his first-phase work on the outside of the mill, and was waiting for planning permission before going ahead with the work on the bedroom and the loo. Meg didn't care whether these plans were passed or not. The mill, as it stood, had been good enough for Henry Waterston — so it was good enough for her.

She was dusting the surfaces of the old bedroom when she heard Matthews's voice calling up to her from the bakery below.

'Coming!' she shouted. With a last look around, she patted the window seat and went down the open stairs to meet him. 'What brings you here? Is it the novelty of my being able to boil an electric kettle now?'

'Just about,' Matthews agreed. 'I have news for you.'

'On the planning application?'

'Not yet. My news is about Henry Waterston's family background — yours too, of course.'

'Excellent!' exclaimed Meg.

'Don't get too excited. It's no more than a possible lead. I didn't know Alison's hobby was researching family trees.' Matthews smiled wryly. 'Indeed I didn't even know that she had a hobby — if I was in the office late, so was she.'

'And?' Meg prompted.

'She has looked through the census returns on computer and traced Henry — and your father — back here to Kirkby. But what excited her is that, in the process, she found that Henry had a sister too.'

'I have an unknown aunt too?'

'Maybe — if she's still alive. Alison traced

that she married a farmer — a tenant farmer — when she was only seventeen. They moved up to Northumbria for a bit, then down to a farm near Darlington. That was about thirty years ago. Then her husband died, and Alison traced her to a house in Darlington itself. That was her address in both 1991 and 2001.'

Matthews held up his hand in warning. 'That was ten years ago, and she's a very old lady now. She was the eldest of the three siblings — herself, your dad, and Henry. Here's that Darlington address.'

With a trembling hand Meg reached for the slip of paper. 'Is she on the phone?' she asked. 'I can't just blunder in on her.'

'Check out directory enquiries. Or simply send a letter. How you tackle it is up to you. And her, of course, if she's still alive.'

Meg stared at the note, smoothing her fingers over the name and address.

'Please tell Alison that I am truly grateful,' she said.

'I already have,' said Matthews.

'Mildred . . . Mildred Collinson. That's an old first name, people don't use it nowadays. Has she any children?'

'One. There was a son shown in the earlier census reports — then he disappeared. That means nothing; he could have got married and moved out of the district. It would take a separate search to find him, and he's not central to the story. If you ever see her, it's a nice opening question to ask.'

Meg folded the note and placed it on the old mantelpiece. 'Thanks ever so much. What about yourself? How's the war going?'

Matthews winced. 'Badly. I just can't trap the lad into conversation, where we could maybe sort things out. As soon as I try any kind of approach, he just walks away. Goes into his bedroom and slams the door.'

'Oh dear,' said Meg. 'Can't Jo make him stay to talk?'

Matthews shook his head. 'It's my problem. I don't want Jo to risk antagonizing the lad by being heavy handed. No, I must find a way through on my own . . . like I said, it's my problem.'

* * *

'Well, Anna,' Matthews said wryly. 'No doubt you will have better-looking dates than me.'

Jo's daughter smiled at him, eyes sparkling. 'I already have,' she said.

'Bet they didn't know Latin,' Matthews teased.

'Boys never do. They're, like, useless. Can I order wine?'

'Too early in the afternoon. You'll have to settle for a Coke.'

Anna pulled a face. 'Once you were my favourite Latin tutor. Now, you're borderline.'

'Story of my life. You must be wondering why I asked you here?'

'No.'

He raised an eyebrow.

'It's Jamie, isn't it?'

Matthews sighed. 'Absolutely. I'm trying to find a way through the minefield he's set for me.'

'Waste of time,' she said. 'Even he doesn't know where he laid the mines — he keeps stepping on them himself. BOOM!' Anna threw her hands up and waved goodbye to imaginary disappearing fragments of her brother.

'A wise Chinese general once said that the first step in any battle is to get to know your enemy better than he knows himself.'

'Was that Chairman Mao?'

'No, General Sun Tzu, about three thousand years before Mao.'

'Cool. So?'

'What can you tell me about your brother — how he thinks, what's driving his dislike of me.'

'You mean what's he like, apart from being the most stupid, boring, and generally useless brother in the world, plus having sweaty feet?'

Matthews grinned. 'That's got me a handle on his weaknesses — but what can you tell me apart from that opening salvo?'

Anna frowned, suddenly serious. 'Jamie loved Dad,' she said after some moments. 'Not like Mum and me. Different, like he was a god, the central figure in a whole new religion — not just our dad.'

'Hero worship?'

Anna's fingers traced channels on the mist which was forming on the side of her chilled can of Coke. 'More,' she said at last. 'I think he is scared.'

'Of your dad?'

'No. Of not being as good as what Dad expected. Of falling short — no, worse than that, of being a total disaster. Dragging down Dad's name.'

Matthews looked at the girl with new respect. 'That's pretty heavy-duty thinking,' he said quietly.

'Dad was physical — big, strong, fast, fearless. Yobs backed off, if he even looked at them. It was written in his face, what he was capable of doing. He got respect. Jamie has built up Dad into a kind of Superman, somebody whom no one can ever match — least of all, himself. And not you. Definitely not you — you're just a pen-pusher, not a soldier.

That's how Jamie sees you.'

'Does he really want to be a soldier, like your dad?'

'He says he does.'

'That's not my question.'

Anna took a long slow sip of Coke, staring out of the bistro window.

'I think he feels that he has to be a soldier, when I'm not even sure that Dad would have wanted him to be one — he knew more than most what a lousy job it is. But Jamie feels that the only way he can honour Dad is to be all the things that Dad was. A clone of a hero. Even if he's not hero material, or even close.'

She looked up. 'Hey, Robert — can I call you Robert? — Jamie's a teenager . . . he's like supposed to be crazy, supposed to hate the world. Don't expect sense from him, he's a mess between the ears right now.'

Matthews nodded at the sense in her words. 'Of course you can call me Robert,' he said absently.

'Do you love Mum?'

The stark words shot at him across the crisp and spotless tablecloth.

'Yes, I do.'

'She's happy. That makes me happy. I think she loves you too — as in really loves you. Maybe even as much as she loved Dad. That's good, but . . . ' Anna winced. 'She's too old to behave like that,' she finished disapprovingly.

Matthews grinned. 'We're never too old to behave like that.'

Anna watched a bead of moisture grow, then run down the side of her can.

'Know what I think?' she said.

'No. Tell me.'

'You have to prove yourself to Jamie. In something physical. Not that you're better than Dad — nobody was, or is. What I meant was that you have to find a way of showing Jamie that you can outlast him, run him into the ground — then show him that it doesn't matter, to come in second. That way, you stop being a pen-pusher, and win his respect. Plus get him thinking again about what he's always believed was important in life — being a winner. Commanding respect.'

Anna looked up and grinned. 'That's the easy bit. If he lets you into his mind, then you're going to have to sort him out. We've tried that — and failed.'

Her smile faded. 'Do you really want to take us on? Make us family? I mean, like, we're seriously dysfunctional. You could have a quieter life.'

'I've had twenty years of a quiet life. I'm coming out of the hermitage.'

By now her eyes were deadly serious. 'That

daughter of yours — the one you lost. Would she have been my age, if she had lived?'

'No. A little older.'

'You're a natural dad,' she said. 'Hey . . . can I have another can of Coke?'

★   ★   ★

It was Andy's idea to drive to Whitby before the summer started and the old fishing town became drowned in day-trippers. Even in mid-May you could only walk along the harbour front at the speed of the slowest visitor.

'Everybody wants to stroll down by the river,' Andy said. This is where the boat trips are, the whelk stalls, the best fish-and-chips shops in Britain. And Dracula, of course.'

'Who?'

'Didn't you know Bram Stoker wrote the original novel here, in Whitby? He was on holiday, a hundred and fifty years ago, and heard an old tale in a harbour pub, about a wild storm blowing on-shore, and a Russian sailing boat, with its sails almost shredded, being driven towards the rocks outside the harbour. The local fishermen ran to the pierhead, to throw a rope, and help survivors. But at the last minute, the boat's skipper took his chance . . . there came a break in the waves and a blast of wind to fill what was left of his sails. He came skidding through the harbour heads, almost on his side, and moored. The locals found the ship full of sailors who had died from a plague picked up in a foreign port, and the skipper was the only man left alive. Stoker listened, with his ears pinned back. Then he went scurrying to his room and wrote his own version of the tale, of a ship driven in by a storm, carrying the coffin of Count Dracula, with a huge guard dog sitting in front of it. And in Stoker's tale the dog was the only one alive, because it was a dead man that they found lashed to the steering wheel . . . '

'Oh my Lord,' said Meg. 'I thought the film was bad enough.'

She slipped her arm round his waist, and felt his own arm reach across her shoulders. She snuggled in, glad there was no market to bake for on a Sunday, delighted to be another tourist taking in the scene — and its legends.

'Want some candyfloss?' Andy asked, as they passed a stall.

'I'm too old.'

'Nobody's ever too old for candyfloss,' he argued.

'You are — as soon as you hate your fingers being made so sticky.'

'All right then.' He changed tack, like a

sailing ship. 'Let me buy you some toasted teacakes then — there's a brilliant old tearoom halfway up Church Street.'

'I'm not hungry.'

'You will be, after we walk up the steps to the abbey. Have you been there before?'

'No. Never.'

'Then you'll love it — start to finish. There's half a dozen old shops in Church Street that sell Whitby jet. It's been mined here, from Roman times.'

'Was jet the stuff Victorians used for mourning jewellery?'

'That's right, the old Queen wore it herself, for about twenty years. It became high fashion, all over the world. It employed thousands in Whitby — mining, and carving.'

'What happened?'

'It fell out of fashion — until the Goths discovered both it and the town in the 1970s. They wore it, and it began to catch on again.'

He gently squeezed her shoulders. 'Let me buy you some.'

'I'll settle for toasted teacakes.'

'I guessed you would,' he said smugly.

They walked up the cobbled street, admiring the window displays, talking, laughing, and moving on. The street turned sharply to the right and began to climb steeply. Andy steered her off this on to a narrow and even steeper lane of cobble slopes and steps.

It was a long, hard climb. Meg paused, panting, leaning on an old cast-iron lamp-post. 'How many steps have we still to go?' she asked.

'A lot,' Andy replied. 'I think they've put in another couple of hundred since I was up here last.'

'You got me here under false pretences,' accused Meg.

'It was the only way.'

'How can I ever trust you again?'

'Time's a great healer. You'll forget. Ready to go on?'

'No. I want you to pick me up and carry me.'

'Drat!' he said. 'I was going to ask you to carry me.'

Arm in arm, they climbed slowly up the unending steps, as the lane curved up the side of the steep hill.

'We'll need oxygen masks if we climb much higher,' Meg warned.

'Only a little further,' Andy said. 'Can you close your eyes, hold my hand, and let me guide you up the last few steps?'

'You won't throw me over? Promise?'

'I don't have enough strength left. Easy ... there's a step in front of you ... now about three paces up the slope, then there's another step . . . ' He slowly led her over the last thirty yards. 'Now,' he said. 'Open your eyes, and look.'

'Oh! How beautiful!' Meg gazed in wonder up at the towering, ruined arches of what had once been one of the most important abbeys in England.

'Now turn and look down at the town,' he instructed.

Meg stared speechlessly at the red rooftops far below, and the silver ribbon which was the river, with tiny boats moored all along its reaches. She slipped her arm round his waist. 'Thank you,' she said at last. 'This is well worth the climb.'

'I knew you'd like it,' he replied. They turned back to study the ruins of the abbey, perched on its high cliff above the grey North Sea.

'Know how it got that way?' he asked.

'Your shoddy building work?'

'Not this time. The old abbey was left open to the storms, when Henry the Eighth nicked the lead from its roof. But it stood like that until one morning in the First World War. Two German cruisers came steaming out of the morning mist, turned and fired a salvo of shells at it. They said afterwards they were aiming at the coastguard station near by. If they did, they were lousy shots. I reckon it was the Kaiser, sending a Yuletide present by half-flattening one of the best-known landmarks in Britain. Merry Christmas!'

He stared up at the gaunt and intricate stonework.

'I'm glad I don't have the job of rebuilding that,' he murmured.

'Andy' she said.

'What?'

'Shut up. Don't spoil the moment.'

'You're Scottish. I'm trying to educate you about our heritage.'

Meg sighed. 'I suppose the only way I can get you to stop talking, is to fill your mouth with toasted teacakes?'

'No,' he replied. 'I have a better idea.'

'What's that?' she asked.

'This,' he said, turning her round and kissing her.

★   ★   ★

The Yorkshire wind teased out a strand of Jo's hair. Robert gently caught it, and felt its delicate softness in his fingertips.

'That tickles,' she said, smiling.

Matthews coloured. 'Sorry. Wasn't thinking,' he apologized.

'What's up with you? There's something on

225

your mind. You've been really quiet, the whole way through the walk. What's bugging you?' Already, Jo thought, she could see into this man's mind and feelings.

'No secret's safe from any woman.' He sighed. 'I've been thinking round a couple of things . . . I was going to tell you later, when I'd made up my mind on both.'

'Tell me now. Maybe I can help.'

Matthews sank back on to the grassy bank, propping himself on elbows. His eyes rose to the blue and white of the sky, watching the clouds drift across.

'I love this place,' he said after a few moments. 'You love this place. It's where you have brought up your family . . . it's home to them.'

'And?'

'And I need to decide what to do with the London lot.'

'What London lot?'

'The partnership. The only work I have ever known — from office boy who made the tea, to eventually stepping into my father's shoes as senior partner. That was his idea — to make me work through every corner of the business, to learn how it ticked, down to the last cog and sprocket. Whatever a sprocket is.'

Jo lay back, shielding her eyes. 'You're

saying that you'll have to go back to London soon, and you're wondering how to break the news to me.'

Matthews smiled. 'Not even close.'

Jo rolled over on to her side and faced him. 'Then what?'

'I'm wondering how to break the news to them.'

Jo frowned. 'What do you mean?'

'The news that I don't think I'm going back. The news that I'm still working out how best to stay here, in Yorkshire. With you.'

Jo studied him. 'Are you serious?'

'I've never been more serious.'

Her heart skipping every second beat, Jo asked: 'Then what are you going to do? You can't just walk out, surely? Not as the senior partner?'

Matthews rolled over on to a single elbow. With his free hand, he reached out and gently touched the tip of her nose.

'All my life, I've done what other people wanted — what they expected of me. Gone to university . . . studied law . . . worked hard to get the best grades going . . . returned to the practice and worked up the ladder . . . shared offices . . . my own office . . . my own secretary . . . became a partner . . . took on the cases where the reputation of the practice was at stake . . . became one of the senior partners

. . . then the most senior partner. Become a clone of my father. Not myself.'

His fingertip absently traced the curve of Jo's cheek; she fought the urge to turn and nibble at it.

'But that's what you wanted, isn't it?' she asked.

'I love the Law. But over these last few weeks I've discovered that I was missing out on life. Locked away in an air-conditioned office, with no home to go to, no family to fight with and to worry about, no one to share my thoughts, my feelings. I'd become as dry as the books on my office shelves . . . without feelings.'

'And now?' Jo said.

'Now I want to live for the day, and take what it offers. I want to live for myself — not the continuity of my father's practice. It can survive without me — it has, for over a month. And I can survive without it. I want to share what's left of my life with you — provided you want to share what's left of your life with me.'

Jo's heart was beating slowly and deeply, like an ancient drum.

'I do,' she said, remembering the last time she had said these words to a man, and all the happiness and grief which had followed. Grief which had all but destroyed her young years.

Only for happiness to return — when she wasn't looking.

'So,' said Matthews. 'There are two options. The first is to abuse the power I have, as senior partner, and open up an office here in Helmsley, then appoint myself as manager. The second is to resign from the practice, and start again on my own. Once more, in Helmsley.'

'The second,' Jo said, instantly.

'That's what I think. It's as Andy says — if you keep the business small, you stay in control of how you spend your life and time. I want to run what he calls 'a lifestyle business', so that I won't make the same mistakes again, as I did when I married Nancy, when work came first and my family second. Never again.'

They watched cloud shadows skim over the meadows.

'You said there was a second problem,' Jo prompted.

'Yes. I need your help.'

'Within reason, you have it.'

'Hear me through, first. It's about Jamie.'

Jo sat bolt upright. 'Have you decided how to handle him?'

'Maybe. It might work — it might not.'

'Tell me.'

'I want to take Jamie away for three days on

my own. On a cure-or-kill experiment. I need you to drive us both across to the Rievaulx Terraces. Jamie and I can pick up the Cleveland Way from there.'

'The long-distance footpath?'

'Yes. We follow it through, sleeping rough when the daylight ebbs. I've done that often on a long walk — not a problem. We walk up through Osmotherley, and across the moors to Guisborough. Then along the stretch from there to the coast at Saltburn. Then down the cliff section through Staithes to Whitby. And down the coast past Robin Hood's Bay and Ravenscar to Scarborough. That's about sixty miles . . . three days' hard walking. The toughest possible, up and down. I need you to pick us up at Scarborough — and keep your mobile phone on, in case we have to bail out from the walk at some stage, for whatever reason. You're our back-up.'

'Jamie's never done anything like that,' Jo said slowly.

'He wants to be a soldier like his dad. The army would have him jogging this — and further — with a heavy survival pack and weapons on his back.'

'I don't want him to be a soldier,' she said softly.

'No more do I. But he has four years left, as a teenager — and that's enough for anybody to change their life's course completely. With a little help.'

'From you?'

'From all of us.'

'You're going to walk him into the ground,' she protested.

'I'm going to walk us both into the ground. Until the only way we can finish the trek, is to become a team. Help each other out.'

'Will it work?' she asked.

Matthews picked up her hand, and kissed her fingertips. 'There's only one way to find out,' he said. 'Unless you have a better idea?'

Long seconds passed.

'That's just it,' sighed Jo. 'I don't.'

*　*　*

'Come in,' Matthews called absently, his head bowed over the scatter of maps and tourist leaflets covering his bed. He glanced up, as the door to the hotel bedroom swung open. 'Oh, it's you, Meg,' he said, surprised. 'I thought it was hotel staff, come to chase me out of my room, and let them tidy up.'

'What on earth are you doing?' Meg asked.

'Planning a walk.'

'It looks like an army HQ, in here.'

'Not a bad image,' Matthews agreed wryly. 'It's a long distance walk that I've been promising myself for years. The Cleveland Way.'

The name meant nothing to her. 'I dropped in because I wanted to see you before I leave for Darlington,' she said.

'Where?' Matthews's mind was still on planning the walk.

'Where Henry Waterston's sister lives. She's replied to the letter I sent her a couple of days ago. She wants to see me. I phoned this morning, and she told me to come straight over and meet her.'

Matthews folded his maps. 'How did she sound?' he asked.

'Really friendly. Both in her letter and on the phone.'

'No niggle about you being Henry's sole beneficiary?'

'Quite the opposite. She's excited about us meeting.'

'Good,' said Matthews. 'Will you be back tonight?'

'Yes — there's dough to get ready for tomorrow.'

He studied her. 'Still enjoying the bakery?'

'Absolutely. The novelty hasn't worn off, and while we're working we're talking through loads of ideas about what we can do to build up the business.' She smiled apologetically. 'One day soon I will be coming to ask your permission to buy a delivery van. Not a new one, Jo insists on that. But we're spilling over what her estate and my hatchback can carry — and we want to do this thing professionally.'

Matthews nodded. 'Best start out as you mean to continue.' He stood up, stretching his cramped back muscles. 'I'll need to see you tonight. I met Paul Chesney in the village this morning. He's not a happy bunny.'

'Because we've decided not to rescue the millstones for a while?'

'Exactly. He said the conservation officer is spitting fire.'

'Oh dear,' said Meg. 'When we still need her permission for everything.'

'That's what Chesney says. He thinks we're foolish to turn down the chance of completing a full reconstruction.' Matthews frowned. 'I don't know why he's so keen on that. It would be more business for him, of course — all the plans and supervising the project. But I feel he's trying to impress the conservation people for some other reason. Maybe there's another big contract on the go.'

'At the end of the day, it's my mill, and my business,' Meg said. 'I doubt I will ever have the millwheels mended — not if it's going to bring in hordes of tourists, to spoil my peace and calm. So we will just have to field his conservation officer, and try to smooth her feathers.'

She sighed. 'I'm more nervous about meeting this old lady. Wish me luck.'

'You'll be fine. Hope you don't find any skeletons in the closet.'

'Why say that? Is there something about Henry that I should know, before I go through to meet his sister?'

'Spoke without thinking,' Matthews apologized. 'No, there's nothing that I'm aware of. All I know about her is from Alison's research. Best of luck, Meg. I hope she can cast some daylight over the Henry Waterston mystery.'

He opened the hotel bedroom door for her.

'Stay safe on the roads,' he said quietly. 'You matter.'

She regarded him quizzically.

'To me, as well as Andy,' he said gently. 'I had a daughter, who would have been about your age. If she had lived.'

★ ★ ★

Glad to get off the busy roads, Meg parked her car. Suddenly, it had become a safe haven in the grim old town, a comfort zone she didn't want to leave. She turned the sun visor down and quickly checked her hair in the mirror, then pushed it up again. Did she really know why she was here?

Other than through blind impulse?

This woman she was about to meet was almost certainly her only living relative. Even as the thought dawned, it rocked her. Until now her mind had been focused on the questions she wanted to ask about Henry, trying to word these in a way which would reassure rather than spook a total stranger.

She had been so preoccupied that it was only now, virtually standing on the woman's doorstep, that she had thought of the woman herself, who was not a total stranger, but her kith and kin. This meeting would take place on very thin emotional ice, for both of them. What if Robert's query was justified about the woman nursing a sense of grievance over Meg receiving all her brother's estate?

Had that made an enemy of her, before they had even met?

Meg glanced nervously at the terraced house. It stood in a neat, tiny garden, and had a freshly painted door and spotless porch. Ridiculously, all she wanted to do now was turn the key in the ignition, and drive away. Taking the coward's route.

She climbed out of the car and took her time to close and lock the door, her heart racing. Then, squaring her shoulders, she set off across the narrow pavement and through the wooden gate, which creaked slightly on dry hinges as she opened it.

It was too late for second thoughts. She read the name on the highly polished brass plate above the letter box. Mrs M Collinson. Like Henry Waterston, she had been an unknown blood relative until only a few days ago — yet she was the one person who might unlock the mystery.

Meg reached out and rang the doorbell.

10

Slow footsteps sounded behind the door, then came the sound of chains being slipped, the main lock turned, then the Yale. The door opened to reveal an old lady, shielding her eyes from the sudden glare.

'Megan? Why — you're so tall! Come in out of the daylight, and let me see you properly.' The old lady stepped back, making space.

Meg stepped inside. Her first impression was of grey gloom and shade everywhere, both in the small hallway and in the room beyond. That, and silence, as if time was standing still.

'Come in, come in.' Her aunt led the way slowly, gesturing for Meg to follow.

Inside the living room were two leather armchairs, with woollen throws over their backs. The walls and every level surface were full of photographs — portraits, small family groups standing self-consciously, a boy sitting astride a small two-wheeler cycle. History of a life, of a mother's memories.

'Sit down,' her aunt said. 'Over there, so I don't have to peer at you against the light . . . that's better. So you're Thomas's girl. I don't see any of him, in you — or even of your mother. I have heard so much about you.'

How did you address an aunt you had only just discovered, Meg wondered. She opted to avoid all names, and hope for the best.

'How could you possibly hear about me?' she asked. 'Until a few months ago, I didn't even know that Henry Waterston existed. And, I'm truly sorry, but until days ago, I knew nothing about you.'

A wry smile flickered on the wrinkled face. 'Thomas? He didn't talk about us then? Nor did your mother, Amy, either?'

'Not a word. I didn't know I had any living relatives.'

'Well, you have,' the old lady said briskly. 'Would you like a cup of tea?'

'Can I help you make it?' Meg asked.

The old lady studied her, then a warm smile grew on her face.

'Eee, lass,' she said broadly. 'Thee an' me are going to get on reet fine. The makings are in the kitchen, and the tray's laid out.'

Meg paused at the kitchen doorway, then found she couldn't speak.

'Out wi'it, lass,' the old lady said kindly. 'And the name is Mildred — we're both of us too old for aunties.'

Meg's words spilled out. 'I've found my

family! It's like Christmas, only better,' she said huskily.

'Found us? Indeed you have. Now get t' tea going.'

Mildred's no-nonsense answer helped to stem the tears, and Meg switched the near-full kettle on. Enough water here to fill the teapot three times over, she thought wryly. Mildred was prepared for a long and detailed family chat. That word again: family.

'I understand you have a son?' she called through.

'Bert — after his granddad on his father's side. He's working in America now, has a family there. Two grandchildren I've got, and another on the way. They want me to visit them, but I'm ower old for flying. So they're coming to see me, when the new baby's fit enough. We skype — you know, with the laptop they sent me. What a gift! I can see them, and watch them grow — even if I've got to talk wi' my best clothes on. Nice girl he's married. He were a mother's boy, cut off my apron strings far too late in life. I'm happy that he's happy. Ah, the tea.'

'You pour,' said Meg. 'It's your house. Going back to my question. Who was always talking about me?'

'Your Uncle Henry. You were the apple of his eye.'

Meg stared at her. 'How could I possibly be that?'

'Milk? Help yourself to sugar, Megan. We've come to what business folk call the real agenda, haven't we?'

'No sugar, thanks.' Meg stirred her tea. 'It was the original agenda,' she conceded. 'I wanted to find out anything I could about Henry Waterston. But right now all I can think of is that I have finally found myself an aunt.'

'And you've come to my door, as Henry always promised you would.'

'What sort of man was he?' Meg asked, sipping tea and waving aside the proffered biscuits.

'I'm going to dunk my biscuit in my tea,' said Mildred. 'This isn't like skype, when I have to be on my best behaviour. What version do you want, then? The public relations one, or a sister's view, with warts an' all.'

'Very definitely warts and all.' Meg smiled. 'I want to know as much about him as I can, then we can start on you.'

'Henry was a decent man: a big, burly, straightforward chap and afraid of nowt on two legs or four. He should have been a farmer — in fact he often helped my man at harvest. Not scared of work, was Henry. He was generous — would give you the shirt off his back if you asked. He and your dad worked the mill between them — Henry doing the grinding and helping in the baking, but working for your dad, the master baker.'

The washed-out blue eyes smiled, looking deep into the past. 'That old mill were in t' family for generations,' Mildred continued. 'We grew up with our dad and his dad working it. We ran wild along the river, guddling trout when we should have been at school. The boys always got belted by our dad — but I got off with it, being a girl. They always said it was their idea, not mine. Even if it wasn't. We were close, the three of us.'

'So, what happened?' Meg asked.

'We grew up,' Mildred answered quietly. 'What else? I left home to get married at seventeen. That started the family rowing, they thought I was ower young. They thought I could have done better. They were wrong — I picked the only man in the world for me, and he treated me like a queen all his life.'

'Then there were other family rows?' Meg prompted.

'More tea? Yes, more rows, but of a different kind. Henry found a lass, and thought the sun shone out of her. Then Thomas found her too. Our dad was dead by then, and our mum before him . . . ' Mildred stopped, and looked intensely at Meg for a few moments, then nodded. 'The two brothers fell out, big style,' she took up the family story, 'happens all over the world, I suppose. Your dad was a right bonny man, good-looking, articulate. He could charm the birds off the trees, an' he charmed Amy away from our Henry, the poor big, blunt, slow-spoken soul.' Mildred hesitated. 'Are you sure you want it, warts an' all?' she asked.

'Warts and all,' confirmed Meg.

'So be it.' Mildred smiled. 'Now I know who you're like,' she said. 'You're the spitting image of our mum. Your looks, your skin tones . . . your hair. She loved that old mill, you know. Used to sit for hours up at the window seat in the big top room, looking out over the trees to the hills.'

'I don't believe it!' Meg exclaimed. 'That's my most favourite place in all the world. And when I'm sitting there, I feel as if there's someone watching over me, and smiling. So quiet and gentle.'

'That'll be our mum,' Mildred said softly. 'That's how she was — and that's where she always sat.' She glanced up, tears in her eyes. 'That feeling you get . . . that's your grandmother, Megan. She sees herself in your face — as I do now.'

Meg felt huge warmth build in her heart. 'I

keep finding different members of my family,' she whispered, 'when all the time I thought I was alone.'

'Oh, we're like weeds, we're everywhere.' Mildred smiled. 'Now do you really and truly want Henry's story, or have you changed your mind? It might spoil your day.'

'I doubt that,' Meg said. 'I love everything I've heard until now.'

'Aye. Might be best to stop — but let's get on wi' it. From what I know, after both of them fell for Amy, the two brothers knocked seven bells out of each other. Henry reckoned he got the better of it most times — but your mum picked your dad from the floor, and went off with him. That stopped the fighting. The two brothers never spoke again. And Henry, bless him, never made the slightest attempt to come between your mum and dad. He stayed his distance — but kept an eye on how your mother was faring. He saw she was happy, and let her be. He was that kind of big-hearted man.'

'Kept an eye on her?'

'After your dad left the mill got neglected. With no bakery there was no need to grind. Henry started working for himself in animal foodstuffs — did well out of that. His work took him all over the country, and when he was near them he'd drive past where your mum and dad lived, hoping to see her out in t'garden. Not like one of these modern stalkers, no threat to it, just a friendly shadow who stayed out of their sight — and their lives. Henry never got over your mum, never looked at another woman.'

Meg sipped tea that had gone cold. 'That's so sad,' she said. 'Is that how he could tell you about her — and me?'

'He was at her funeral — out beyond the edges of the crowd.'

'I never saw him.'

'He took good care you didn't — said there was enough grief already in your life.'

Above them, on the mantelpiece, an old clock ticked. To one side of it was a framed modern photograph of a middle-aged man, his arm round a smiling younger wife, and two children lined up in front of them — looking as if they wanted to be off playing somewhere else. On the other side a much smaller, faded, black-and-white photograph showed a young boy, astride a bike, the boy who might just have become that middle aged man. Over the bridge of time, the same time that had been measured by that clock.

'So his interest in me was because I was my mother's daughter?' Meg asked.

The clock ticked on. And on. Mildred carefully put down her cup into the china saucer and stared quizzically at Meg.

'If that's how you want to see it,' she answered at last.

The hair on Meg's neck and arms rose in painful goose-bumps. She rubbed her arms gently. 'Is that the way I should see it?'

Mildred's eyes drifted to the photo of her family in distant America.

'Happen so,' she said. 'At t'end of the day, it maybe was.'

'But that's not how he saw it?' Meg prompted quietly.

Minutes passed, then Mildred's calm eyes came back to her.

'No, he saw it different,' she replied.

'How different?'

'He believed, all his life, that you were his child. That he was your father.'

Meg's mind went numb. Then became a drum, on which Mildred's words beat endlessly. They explained so much.

'And was he?' she ultimately asked.

The faded blue eyes never wavered. 'We'll never know for sure, because you were early-born. From what I know of your mum — my good friend Amy — I would doubt it. But love is primal, intense. It knows no laws, or boundaries, so maybe she did have an earlier fling with Henry. And if she didn't, then the grief that comes from losing out can drive a man to madness, into believing something with all his heart — even if it's based on dreams, not fact. Maybe that's how it was with Henry. All he ever wanted was to spend his life with his Amy. That didn't happen . . . he came second best. But, fact or dreaming, Henry never wavered in his belief that you were his daughter. So yes, he did watch over Amy — that love was real, and he cared for her deeply — but he were watching over you as well. Over every month and year of your life, always from the shadows. It was you he told me about when he came back from Amy's funeral. After Amy's death, he was trying to make up his mind whether he should speak to you. Or if what he had to tell you, would scare you stiff. He died, still wondering, not wanting to hurt you.'

'I never knew . . . '

'How could you? But he went to his grave thinking that you were the child that he and Amy should have had.'

'And was I?' The question returned, unbidden.

'If it helps, I'll say that I doubt it. But if you want the truth, then I simply do not know . . . '

*　*　*

The wind is never still, over the Yorkshire moors — not even at night. Matthews drowsed, tired out after a hard day's walking, listening to it rustling through the grass and heather, while the night stars glittered high above his head.

He became conscious that the boy was twisting and turning in his sleeping bag, at the other side of the path.

'Are you all right, Jamie?' he asked quietly.

A grunt. Then a silence. Then: 'No.'

'What's up?'

'Can't get comfortable. There's rocks and stones beneath me.'

'That's easy cured.' Matthews unzipped his own sleeping bag and began to hunt through his pack for the Swiss Army knife. 'Hang on,' he said. 'Let me cut you a mattress fit for a king.'

'Don't bother. I'm fine.'

'You don't *have* to be uncomfortable. See, this is how you deal with that . . . ' Matthews worked busily with the sharp knife in the dark, feeling for the thick heather stems, then cutting through them. After a few minutes' work, he had enough spread along the ground to make a thick and stiffly sprung mattress.

'Put your sleeping bag over that,' he said. 'This is how the gypsies get a good night's sleep. They lie on a bed made of heather and bracken — but it's too early in the year for bracken. Your sleeping bag should take the jaggy bits out of the equation. Here, let me help you.'

He spread the warm sleeping bag carefully on top of the heather platform.

'Try that,' he said. 'I'll buy a hat in the first village we pass through tomorrow, then eat it, if you aren't more comfortable.'

The boy shivered. 'I'm cold,' he said. 'Too cold to sleep.'

'Here.' Matthews slipped out of his warm jacket. 'Put that over your own fleece, and climb back into the sleeping bag.'

'That's not right.' Jamie said awkwardly. 'Now you'll get cold.'

'I'm used to it,' Matthews lied, wondering if he should cut some smaller sprigs of heather and stuff his own sleeping bag with them as extra insulation. That might work in theory, but he doubted it would be comfortable, it also brought the risk of picking up deer ticks. Better to tough it out.

They wriggled back into their bags and zipped them up.

'What's that noise?' asked Jamie.

'A curlew. There's lots of them on the moors.'

'Sounds scary. Like a ghost going whoo — whoo — whoo.'

'Never heard a ghost.' Matthews smiled in the dark. 'But I've heard plenty of curlews. With luck, you'll maybe see some in the early morning.'

A pause. 'How early?' Jamie asked.

'When daylight wakens us. Pretty early, I guess. We can have our breakfast at the stream down there.'

'I'm not brushing my teeth in that,' warned Jamie.

'OK. I won't tell tales to your mum — if you don't tell tales about me.'

Another pause. 'Deal,' said Jamie sleepily.

The heather bed was unbelievably comfortable. The boy wriggled luxuriously. One in the eye for his sister, he thought. He was only here because she had taunted him that he didn't have the bottle to make the trip — or the stamina to complete it. He would prove her wrong — or burst.

And Matthews, now that he had no option but to get to know the man, was a decent guy. Not stiff and pompous at all. In fact, more at home in the wilds than he himself would ever be. That deserved respect.

'Thanks,' he said.

It wasn't a big word, but it took a lot of saying. Then he was asleep.

Matthews heard, and smiled quietly into the dark. Progress. But, without his jacket, and now that the sleeping-bag had cooled down from his leaving it, he himself was shivering from the cold. He shuddered. No gain without pain, he quoted to himself.

Stoically, he set himself to wait for dawn. Long before it came, he was asleep.

★　★　★

'How did your meeting go with the old lady?' asked Jo.

'Mind-blowing,' Meg replied, thinking there was much of what she'd discovered that she couldn't tell a living soul — not even Jo. 'I found myself a real live aunt — a wonderful old character. We had a great time, but I think she's lonely. It was three hours before I managed to escape. Even then, I had to promise to come back and see her, which I will. How about you? Have you heard from Robert and Jamie yet? How long have they been on their marathon?'

'This is their second day,' Jo replied. Although exhausted, she hadn't slept a wink the night before, worrying not just about Jamie but about Robert too. Had he bitten off more than he could chew, to win her boy round?

They worked systematically preparing the dough to be left to prove overnight. At the far side of the bakery old Fred slumped morosely in a chair. Andy had brought him over to check on his apprentices, then left to work on another job in nearby Malton. For the last half-hour Fred had barely spoken.

Now he cleared his throat. 'Happen you can do wi'out me,' he said.

Meg stopped kneading, surprised. 'What do you mean?' she asked.

Fred tugged at an already-stretched ear. 'The pair o' thee are doin' away reet fine,' he said. 'Past needin' me.'

'Stuff and nonsense!' declared Jo.

Fred sniffed. 'Women learn faster,' he said. 'The pair of thee have learned me out of a job There's nowt left t' teach.'

'We're thinking of branching into celebration cakes,' said Meg. 'You know, birthday and wedding cakes. Maybe even Christmas cakes.'

Fred brightened. 'I cin teach thee that,' he said. 'Was a reet dab hand at cakes when I were young.'

'Then you've still got work to do with us — after all, we're only apprentices,' Meg said. Then she stopped kneading as a car drew in over the gravel outside.

'Who's that?' she asked, peering through the bakery windows.

'A fancy clogs,' said Fred. He shifted his

251

weight on to his other scrawny buttock, leaning forward on his stick.

'Don't just sit there. Open the door,' scolded Jo.

'Has thee lost tha servant?' Fred shot back.

'We're kneading dough. You're quick enough to complain, when we stop to chat about something.'

'Dough needs to be worked,' confirmed Fred.

'Well, we're working it. You answer the door.'

Fred grumbled and shuffled out. Sunlight flooded the bakery, then vanished as the door was closed again. 'Says he wants t' speak t' thee,' said Fred.

'Who does?' asked Jo, pounding dough.

'Him. T' fancy-clogs.'

'Lord save me,' Jo exclaimed. She scraped flour and dough off her hands.

'Come through, please — where we can see you,' Meg called.

A middle-aged man came smiling out of the shadows. 'James Conroy,' he said. 'But Fancy Clogs will do. Am I speaking to the ladies who bake for the local markets? They told me I would find you here.'

'Ladies?' muttered Fred, shuffling back to his seat.

'Ignore him — he came with the

252

woodworm in the furniture,' said Meg.

'Nice set-up you have,' said Conroy, eyes missing nothing. 'Old ovens too . . . traditional, wood-burning.'

'And bread lik' it used to taste,' said Fred.

'That's why I'm here. I bought some as I was passing, last week — then came back to buy some again on Monday. Nice texture, nice flavour. Are you fully organic?'

'From the flour to the loaf,' said Meg. 'And locally sourced ingredients. We have a hard taskmaster.'

'That's me,' said Fred. 'I taught 'em bread, like it were allus made.'

'And that's how it tastes,' said Conroy. 'Quality like that is wasted on a market stall.' He came over, reaching for his wallet, and took out a business card. '*Natural Eating*,' he said. 'It's an organic foodstuffs shop I run in York — out at Monks' Bar. We've been there for fifteen years. We're losing our bakery supplier — he's closing down, to retire — and I'm searching for a replacement. I'd like a pilot run for the plain white you make. Let's say a month, at ten dozen a day. If the quality holds, I will go up to twenty dozen a day. Maybe more. Can you manage ten, for starters?'

Meg shot a look at Jo; they were already working pretty flat out.

Jo nodded imperceptibly.

'We can do that,' said Meg, wondering how they would fit in the extra work — and where she might find a good used van to carry it.

'You could be what I'm looking for, a small-scale outfit focused on traditional baking. But the proof's in the pudding — or the bread in this case. Can you deliver as routine? Can you keep up the quality of your loaf, under pressure? No point in interviews — anybody can promise anything in interviews. A pilot run is the only way to test out the product. If I'm happy, it could be a long-term contract for us both. But let's review the position in a month's time. And I'll need certification that your loaf is purely organic.'

'Not a problem,' said Jo. 'We've been organic from the start, but never marketed it as such.'

'Good. Now, if this works out, I will be wanting not just plain white but a full replacement range of bread from you, to replace what I'm losing, and where I've built up an established demand. Can you do wholemeal, both plain and seeded, wholemeal with oats and honey, Greek olive bread, rye with caraway seeds? Tiger bread? Can you tackle these?'

'No problem,' said Fred. 'Who was your supplier?'

'Andrew Jones, in Ripon.'

'Closing down, is he?'

'In a couple of weeks. He gave me early warning, to let me look for a replacement supplier. He's been baking for us for the last ten years, but has nobody to take over the business. His son is in computers.'

'That's the way it goes,' Fred said gravely. 'Young have no interest.'

'Quite. So we will start with plain white batch? Ten dozen. Can you manage that from Monday?'

'Monday it is,' said Fred.

Conroy smiled. 'It's a real opportunity for you,' he said. 'I'm going on gut-hunch, but you must hold that quality and be reliable. My address is on the card — any problems, phone me. I'll run you alongside Jones's bread for a week. Then you take over. So I will need that full range of bread in two weeks time . . . '

'Fine,' said Fred.

'Until then,' said Conroy. 'Remember, any problems . . . '

'Don't worry. You'll get t' best bread in Yorkshire.' Fred nodded, and checked his watch.

'I'll settle for that,' said Conroy.

When he'd left, the three of them looked at each other.

'Can we do the extra white?' Jo asked.

'No choice — we'll have to,' said Meg, her legs suddenly weak.

'We never planned on this,' said Jo. 'It's going to double our output.'

'No more dog-walking,' said Meg.

'Well . . . let's see,' said the canny Jo. She turned to Fred. 'What's Tiger Bread?' she asked.

'Damned if I know,' he replied.

'But you said we can do it!' Jo exploded. 'What about Greek Olive?'

'Nivver heard of it,' Fred said cheerfully.

The two women looked at each other speechlessly.

'Fred? What have you got us into?' Meg demanded.

'A decent contract,' he replied smugly.

'Not if we can't bake the fancy bread he wants!'

'Oh we will,' said Fred. 'Get that dough finished, then we're int' car and off to Ripon. There's nivver been a decent baker yet from Ripon — tho' plenty thought they were. Jones? At least he's still open, an' he's still bakin'.'

He rose, leaning heavily on his stick. 'We're heading off to buy one loaf of each,' he said. 'Let me taste a slice of it an' I can tell you how he's made the bread. Then we can ask him about his own supplies — the Greek olives an' stuff . . . mebbe buy thim cheap, if he's closing down.'

'Fred! You're a heartless old pirate!' exclaimed Jo.

He looked surprised. 'Common sense,' he said. Then with his hand, he waved them to greater efforts.

'C'mon,' he said. 'Git workin'. We've a visit to make.'

* * *

Meg sank wearily into her chair; another morning's delivery run had been completed, which meant there were a few short hours of rest and recuperation, before she must start on the dough for tomorrow. Not for the first time she wondered how Jo could keep up this pace of work and still have the energy to walk dogs and run a family.

She had taken to nodding off for half an hour, while she had the mill to herself. Herself, and her gentle grandmother, she now knew. There was a small smile on her face as she drifted to sleep in the comfortable old chair.

That was how Andy found her, an hour later. He grinned, and moved a couple of strands of hair away from where they had fallen over her face. In her sleep, she grumbled. He tiptoed through to the kitchen, and gently ran water into the electric kettle and plugged it in. Soon the kettle came to life.

That wakened her. Meg sat up with a start.

'Never fails,' he complained to the kitchen sink. 'Put kettle on, then open coffee jar, and even corpses come to life.'

Meg scrubbed at her eyes. 'When did you come in?' she asked.

'Three hours ago,' he lied, and smiled as she frantically checked her watch.

'Don't do that,' she said weakly. 'I thought I'd missed out on the dough. I hope you're making two mugs of coffee?'

'All organized,' he said. 'Waiting for the water boiling.' He studied her, noting the dark smudges beneath her eyes. 'How are you coping with these early starts?' he asked.

'Not very well.'

'Hang in there. Your body soon gets used to its new timetable.'

'It has no choice.' She yawned.

'Sorry I didn't look in, yesterday,' he said. 'I had a beast of a job . . . the kind that takes brute force and refuses to listen to reason. How did your visit go, to your new-found aunt Mildred?'

Meg stared at the floor. 'Just Mildred,' she

said slowly. 'She wants no truck with being called aunt.'

'Nor should she,' Andy said. 'Here's your coffee. I'm in my working gear. Can I sit down, or will I go and perch on the sink.'

Meg flapped a weak hand to the other chair. 'Boy, do I need that coffee,' she said, savouring the smell, then the first wonderful taste.

Andy's frown deepened. 'What's ado?' he asked.

Meg shook her head.

'Fallen out with Jo?'

'As if!' Meg snorted.

'Oh, even best friends fall out, from time to time. Then what is it?'

'Can't tell.'

'Why not?'

Meg ran her free hand through her hair. 'Because,' she said. 'I can't tell you because . . . ' Her voice drifted into silence.

Andy waited patiently. The old clock ticked slowly and heavily away.

Then Meg turned to him. 'What do you do if your whole world is turned upside down by something?' she asked him bleakly.

'Talk about it, to someone close. Someone you can trust.'

Meg's eyes drifted away. More minutes passed, then she sighed. Just now there was nobody in the whole world closer to her than Andy. If she couldn't blurt out the story of Henry Waterston's obsession to him — could she tell anyone?

It took less than three minutes, to spin the tale. Even though there were lots of pauses between the sentences. Finished, she buried her face into her mug.

'So?' asked Andy.

'That changes everything,' she said.

'No it doesn't. The mill's still here. You're still here. It hasn't changed in any way — nor have you. Are you any different a person, from who you were last week? Grown another head? Murdered the village vicar? Taken to drink?'

Numbly, she shook her head at his gentle teasing.

He came over and tenderly lifted her chin up. 'There's two options, as I see it. Either Henry Waterston was your dad or Henry Waterston was wrong. Even Mildred doesn't know for sure — and these were her family, her people. If he was your dad, then he loved you with all his heart, and left you everything. If he was wrong, then he behaved like a real gentleman. Kept his distance, didn't rock the boat, didn't make life difficult for anybody. Took all the pain on himself.'

He reached down, and gently kissed her

nose. 'Seems to me, old Henry was a decent bloke. Either way, you can be proud of him. And, either way, it doesn't wipe out your childhood. You were happy with your parents, and the love you got from them was real. So the bottom line is this: they were three decent people and, whatever the truth was, they took it to the grave with them. Where it can't touch you now.'

With his fingertip he gently touched her brow. 'Now, here's the important bit to grasp. Whichever couple were your parents, you're the same Meg you've always been. You are what you've made of the life you were given and, as of last week, that was good enough to have me wondering if I should be asking you to marry me.'

'You what?' Meg exploded.

'Calm down,' he said. 'Was only wondering. A Yorkshireman can wonder for months on end, before he makes up his mind. Why, I could run off with the village postmistress, once I decide — '

'Don't you dare!' cried Meg.

He waved a placating hand. 'OK, she's too old to run. We could shuffle off into the sunset.'

'If you do, I will never post another letter. Not in all my life.'

Andy threw up both hands. 'There you

are,' he said. 'The future of the British postal system hangs in the balance; my choice, deciding. The responsibility is almost too much to bear.'

His blue eyes danced.

'I have multiple camera CCTV running,' Meg lied. 'Turn that over in your devious Yorkshire mind. I have all of this on tape.'

'Rats!' he sighed. 'Then I suppose I had better get it over with.'

From outside came the unmistakable sound of a car coming over the gravel of the track, then a second one. Doors banged.

'Hey oop!' said Andy softly. 'We have visitors.'

He walked over to the kitchen window and looked down.

'Well, well,' he said. 'Paul Chesney. And he has company — the conservation officer . . . '

11

The conservation officer seemed pleasant enough, Meg decided. Led by Chesney, she inspected the external repair work, the bakery and its ovens, the top bedroom where they briefly discussed the planned modernization, and the machine-house section of the mill, with its millstones, drive rods and ancient hopper.

At the end of the grand tour they were left standing in the granary, where once the sacks of wheat and corn had been hoisted by pulley to be emptied down the hopper and its chute on to the rumbling millwheels below.

At last Chesney stopped talking and looked round for support.

'Well,' said Andy, 'I buy into Paul's belief that the mill machinery is rescuable. But there's one section of the gears that's worrying me.' He turned to the officer. 'You've probably seen dozens of them, but the water power is turned round several directions into driving power by gears. The water-wheel drives a shaft that comes directly through the fabric of the building to rotate a pitwheel which meshes with the crownwheel, which meshes with the oak mainshaft. It's the spurwheel on that mainshaft which drives the vertical shaft that turns the mill-stones — so it's a key part.'

'I'll take your word for that,' the conservation officer said.

Andy grinned. 'Took me days to figure that out,' he said. 'But I think we've two potential problems. First, the spur-wheel looks badly damaged — and it's not going to be easy to cast a replacement. Second, and much worse, I can't find any gear controls — there's usually some braking or damping mechanism — but that's completely missing.' He shrugged. 'We might have to invent these controls again.'

'Nonsense,' said Chesney. 'It's a primitive mill. They would control power simply by raising or lowering the sluice gates.'

'Too crude. Once these millwheels get turning, they're so heavy they develop their own dynamic. That could leave them fighting against the driving power of the waterwheel, and chewing the gears. I think we should go down and have another look at it, Paul. I'd welcome a second opinion there . . . because this could be crucial to any decision.'

'It's mucky, down there. I'm in my work suit.'

'So am I,' Andy said cheerfully.

Almost casually, he took Chesney's wrist in his hand. Meg saw his knuckles whiten as he applied pressure, and the look of surprise turn to one of pain on Chesney's face. 'Let's leave the ladies to themselves for a couple of minutes, and check these gears,' Andy said. His eyes flicked to Meg, then to the official.

Meg read the signal instantly: *I'll deal with him; you handle her.*

The conservation officer watched them go, a slight smile on her face. 'Men and machines,' she said. 'Boys in long trousers!'

'Would you like to come downstairs for a cup of tea?' Meg asked.

'Tea would be lovely.'

A few minutes later, in the comfort of the armchairs, the officer sipped and looked up. 'Regardless of this technical problem of Andy's, Paul seems to think you are still open to persuasion on the full reconstruction?'

'He has been pushing hard for that,' Meg replied.

'But you're not too keen yourself — hence the need to push?'

Meg sipped tea, buying a few seconds' time. 'There is nothing I want more than to restore as much of the mill as I can,' she said. 'I love this old building, and want to put it back to rights, then live in it. I'm perfectly happy to leave the top floor as it is, without modernization.'

'There should be no problem with the proposed changes — they don't affect either the nature or the appearance of the building. If your plans are passed by the planners, my approval would be automatic.'

'And the bakery?'

'An important element of the reconstruction. I'm delighted to have the old ovens restored and working again.'

Knowing that the next few words were crucial, Meg set her cup down, and walked to the window. She became conscious that the conservation officer had followed her, and was standing at her side. In silence, they looked out at the sunlight-dappled leaves outside.

'So our problem is the millwheels,' the official said quietly.

Meg took a deep breath. 'I don't have the time, or the money, to restore these millwheels.'

'There are grants available.'

'OK,' Meg said, glad to stop fencing. 'I should have said that I don't have the time, or the desire, to restore the millwheels.'

'Because?'

'Because I don't need them for the bakery business. And I hate the thought of turning the mill into a tourist attraction. A constant stream of the public coming to see the working millstones would destroy the peace of this lovely place. It would take away the very reason I want to restore the mill, and live here.'

They stood in silence, broken only by the

sound of the river outside.

'That I can fully understand,' the conservation officer replied. 'Does this mean that you would never consider restoring the millwheels?'

Meg hesitated. 'Never is too strong a word. I do like the idea of grinding my own flour one day. But, right now all my money and my energy is going into launching a bakery business. Once I see the bakery successful, I would like to take soundings with my market, to check whether grinding our own flour would increase demand for our bread. I can't see any point in restoring, for the sake of restoring — without knowing if you would ever recoup the money invested in the project.'

That drew a smile. 'Spoken like a true businesswoman.'

The moment of truth. 'If we stop short of restoring the millwheels, would the rest of the repair work be blocked?' Meg asked quietly.

A look of surprise. 'Why should it?'

'Paul hinted that you weren't too pleased, that your preference was for the entire reconstruction to go through.'

'The second part is correct. Not the first.' The official returned to her chair, frowning. 'Yes I would prefer a complete reconstruction — that's always the main objective of any conservation. But it's also important to me to ensure that the building is preserved, repaired

. . . lived in. So while I have yet to fully decide, I believe half a loaf is better than none — if you will pardon the awful pun. I am inclined to support what you are doing, and encourage you to think again about the millstones at some future date.'

Meg felt a huge weight lift. 'Paul has been pushing so hard,' she sighed. 'I was scared we would annoy you, and lose your support.'

'I'd be a poor official if I let disappointment influence my decision.'

The conservation officer stood up. 'Off the record,' she said. 'Paul Chesney is one of our best up-and-coming young architects. But he still thinks he's living and working in London. He's too pushy. Too much in a hurry . . . and I suspect the downturn in housebuilding and extensions has hit his business hard. Before it, we were on the fringe of the long-distance commuter belt to London, a high-income market with lots of design and improvement work going on. Now, London commuters have melted away and the housing market has taken a hit from which it might take five or even ten years to recover.' She paused. 'Paul is pushy, because he needs the business. That doesn't stop him from being an excellent architect.'

'He has done a lot of good things for us,' agreed Meg.

'Then be grateful — but exercise your common sense.'

Meg smiled. 'That's exactly what I'm doing,' she said.

The conservation officer rose. 'Now we had better get down and rescue Paul,' she said. 'Before Andy does him serious damage.' She smiled. 'Men can be so primitive . . . but there's a time and a place where that helps. As it did now.'

Meg grinned. 'Let's hope he's only slightly killed Paul,' she said.

★ ★ ★

High above the two toiling figures a seagull glided effortlessly in the updraught from the cliffs. Below, endless ranks of grey waves surged around the rocks, leaving white lace-works of foam when they retreated. In the entire bleak landscape, under that vast sky, these were the only humans.

Matthews panted harshly, the muscles of his legs on fire with the constant descents and long steep climbs. At times he felt that he would have to stop, flop down in the mud, and sleep.

He struggled on. This exhaustion was crucial to his plan.

The boy was dropping further and further

behind. Head down, thumbs hooked in the straps of his backpack, his arms were too weary to swing. Under Matthews's watchful eye, Jamie stumbled, and stopped, panting.

Matthews went back. 'We need to hydrate,' he said. 'Which is a fancy way of saying we need to drink some water.'

'Not thirsty.'

'Are you sweating.'

Jamie looked up, puzzled. 'Not any more,' he said.

'That means you're dehydrated. Nothing left to sweat out. Think how tennis players gulp drinks, between each game. If you stop sweating you stop thinking, then feel tired and sluggish. Come on, let's take a five-minute break.'

They flopped down beside the track.

'Don't glug,' warned Matthews. 'That water has to last all afternoon.'

'Sorry. It was more than half-gone already.'

'OK, relax. There's an emergency bottle of water in my pack.'

'Cheers,' The boy forced himself to sip, rather than empty his large plastic bottle. 'How far have we walked now?' he asked.

Matthews checked his map. 'We're here,' he said, pointing. 'I reckon we've done about fifty miles.'

'How far to go?'

'Seven, maybe eight.'

Jamie pulled a face.

'We're doing two miles an hour, so that's about four hours' walking. Then your mum will be waiting for us. Fish and chips all round, and as much tea or Coke as you want to drink. And school on Monday.'

'Can't wait,' said Jamie.

'For going back to school?'

Jamie looked up, grinning. 'I meant the fish and chips,' he said.

'You had me worried.'

Through the ground beneath them, they could feel the thud of each breaking wave.

'Bet the end of the world looks like this,' said Jamie. 'Just cliff, and sea, and sky. What do you call those islands, off the point of South America?'

'Tierra del Fuego, isn't it? Across the straits from Cape Horn?'

Jamie twisted grass between his fingers. 'My Dad was down there. Some sort of exercises, after the Falklands War. He was a hero, you know . . . ' His voice tailed off.

At last, thought Matthews.

'A bit frightening that — to live up to,' he said casually.

It brought a quick look, but no reply.

Matthews picked a stem of grass and studied it. 'Sons don't have to follow fathers,' he said quietly. 'It's taken me all my life to find that out. We're not born to be . . . simply echoes of what our fathers did. Mine won every prize in Oxford — I got a first, and thought I was a failure because there were two other guys far brighter than me, and they vacuumed up all the prizes between them.'

Silence.

'It's right for us to take pride in what our fathers did, and what they achieved. Celebrate their life, acknowledge that they were brilliant at what they did. But we don't have to follow them, or match them — what does that prove? Does the world really need two Supermen, or two Captain Marvels?'

He stood up, aching in every muscle. 'Let's move. If we sit much longer we'll seize up. Better to go, before we chill.'

They hoisted on their backpacks and started the long steep climb.

'Seriously, what sort of career would your dad have wanted you to follow?' Matthews asked.

'Dunno.'

'Do you honestly think he would have wanted you to be a soldier, like he was? And maybe be killed, like he was? Leaving your mum and Anna on their own, and hurting worse than ever?'

Silence.

Panting heavily, they reached the top of the hill and climbed over a stile that bridged a field fence. For a few blessed yards the coastal path ran across flat ground, before plunging steeply down into the next fold of land.

They reached the bottom of the slope, and slithered through clinging mud and boggy ground. 'Everybody is born different, capable of following different paths,' said Matthews. 'In fact, the world depends on us doing exactly that — if everybody was the same, we'd be in a right old mess. So, however much we admire our fathers, we are allowed to be different. With complete freedom to choose. So, try to be yourself — not what you think other people want you to be. Be a soldier, if you must. But remember, you might make a better fireman, or a journalist — or even a better barrister.'

A wry smile appeared on the boy's muddy face. 'Does the world really need another one of those?' he asked.

Matthews grinned. 'Neat! With a mind like that, maybe you will be a lawyer. Doesn't change my advice — step out of your father's shadow.'

'And Anna?'

'If she gets the grades I will see that she goes to college.'

'And Mum?'

'If I make her unhappy, I will pick the heaviest stick I can find, and hand it over to you. To beat me with.'

Long silence. They paused, gasping, halfway up the slope.

'I'm not trying to be your dad,' Matthews wheezed. 'I'm a different kind of man, a lawyer, not a brilliant soldier. I bow to him. He made your mum happy. He's not here now. I want to try to make her happy again. Give every day of my life to doing just that — if you and Anna let me.'

'What if I want to go to college too?' panted Jamie.

'Once you find your path, I will be there, behind you. Encouraging you, urging you on, helping in any way I can. I owe that to your dad.'

'Why?'

'Because he's gone. And I'm trying to finish the job he started, as best I can.'

They struggled up the last steep slope of the path, to find themselves on the shoulder of yet another headland and facing a huge six-step stile.

'I'm knackered,' Jamie gasped, head down. 'Can't climb that.'

Matthews forced himself up the slippery wooden steps. He reached the narrow platform at the top, and stood, his legs quivering. They were both at the end of their tether, he knew. Turning unsteadily, he held the top rail with one hand and reached down.

'Come on, Jamie,' he said. 'You can do this.'

'Says who?'

'Says me. We have five miles still to go for that fish supper. And we're not going to make it unless we work as a team. I'm knackered too.'

He reached further down. 'Ready?'

The boy's hand reached up hesitantly, then closed on his.

'Ready,' said Jamie, and began to climb.

★   ★   ★

Amid the busy tables at *Mother Hubbard's* in Scarborough, the two long-distance walkers stood out like sore thumbs. You can wash faces and hands, and comb hair — but the legs of their jeans and even their shirts were liberally daubed with mud.

'The coastal path?' the waitress asked.

Jamie nodded. 'We've done over fifty miles of that,' he said proudly.

'Yes — we get a lot of the walkers in here,' she said. 'Enjoy your meal.'

The two men wolfed into the king-sized helpings of beautifully fried fish and chips set before them. A bit of fresh fish on her fork, Anna looked at her mother.

'You would think they were starving,' she said.

'We are,' said Robert, indistinctly, cramming another bite of bread into a mouth which was already full.

Jo grimaced. 'Two days away from civilization, and look at them.'

'I'm still hungry,' said Jamie. 'Can I have more chips?'

Nobody left much apart from the pattern on the plate.

'We've got a surprise for you,' said Jo. 'Due any time.'

'Is it edible?' asked Matthews. 'Fancy another pot of tea?' He waved over to the waitress without waiting for an answer.

'No, to both questions,' she sighed. 'Whatever happened to the elegant and refined lawyer I used to know?'

'We dragged him down to our level,' said Jamie. 'Any chance of another plate of scones and cakes?'

Anna grinned at her mother. Job done, she thought, and preened herself, for being the one who had suggested it. 'So, when are you getting married?' she asked. 'And will I be the bridesmaid?'

Jo blushed. 'I'm still waiting on being asked,' she said.

'Wait until I get my mouth empty,' mumbled Matthews.

'Right now there should be a roll on the

drums,' said Jamie. 'Then a spotlight shining down from the ceiling to highlight the happy couple.'

'Don't you dare,' said Jo. 'I'll leave the place.'

'And embarrass Robert?' Anna demanded.

'Who said you can call him Robert?' Jamie countered.

'If you grow up, we can both call him Robert,' she replied.

Matthews waved a placating hand. 'Call me Robert, both of you,' he said, smiling. He had the growing, warm feeling that the rest of his life would be lived amid the noise and arguments and endless dynamics of this family, a feeling which filled the empty vacuum which had waited years for a commitment such as this.

He reached across the table to take Jo's hand gently. He felt her fingers quietly press against him and return the silent message of their love.

'Jo Chisholm,' he said softly. 'Will you marry me?'

'Hey!' protested Anna. 'What about something on how she is the love of your life, how your life has been dull and empty until you found her?'

'OK. Add that in,' sighed Matthews.

'And what about the bit . . . you know, how

you're going to spend the rest of your life, just trying to make her happy,' suggested Jamie.

'Add that in as well. Any other clauses?'

'Like she's the most beautiful woman you have ever known,' suggested Anna.

'And the best cook in Ryedale?' offered Jamie.

'And . . . ' started Anna.

'Enough,' said Jo. 'The answer's yes.'

'I was just warming up,' mourned Anna. 'Now you've gone and ruined my proposal.'

Matthews lifted Jo's hand towards his lips, and gently kissed it.

'For as long as I live,' he said quietly, 'I will try to make you happy.'

'You have, already,' whispered Jo.

'See — he said it better than you did,' Anna told Jamie. 'The happy bit.'

Jamie looked around the restaurant, where already some smiling faces were turned towards them. 'Should we announce it, like?' he asked. 'Get a round of applause from the other punters?'

A tall shadow loomed over him. 'A round of applause for what?' it asked.

Matthews tore his eyes from Jo, to find Meg and Andy standing there.

'They're your surprise,' said Jo. She looked up at Meg, her face radiant and young. 'We're going to get married!' she said.

'That's funny,' said Andy. 'So are we.'

'It was a straight choice between me and the village post-mistress,' explained Meg. 'I won.'

Jo frowned. 'We don't have a village postmistress,' she said.

Meg turned to Andy. 'You've done it again! Got me under false pretences!'

'You'll get over it,' said Andy. He waved the waitress over. 'Can we have two more fish teas, please?' he asked. 'She's paying . . . '

*　*　*

Somewhere south of the grey urban skyline, lay the outer sprawl of London. And somewhere beyond that, Meg knew, Robert Matthews was dotting his final i's and crossing his final t's for his father's legal firm. Someone else, like her, who would be itching already to get back to the high blue skies and the restless breezes of Yorkshire.

'There you are,' said Andy, brushing aside the grass clippings and straightening up. 'That tidies up the grave for a bit.'

Easily, he rose from his knees and stepped back to stand beside Meg. His hand reached out, and closed over hers. Together they looked at the plain grey headstone, so much like the man himself: nothing fancy; fewest possible words.

Meg read them: HENRY WATERSTON, 1939 — 2011. And that was that — nothing about beloved son, or brother of . . . He had died a recluse, unloved by anyone. Setting aside only enough to cover the most basic of headstones. And leaving everything else to her.

She was conscious of something tickling the side of her nose and, raising her finger, she absently brushed it off.

When she looked, her finger was wet with tears.

Meg bit back the sob which rose in her throat. Felt the gentle pressure from Andy's hand. She was not alone. She looked down at the small bunch of flowers in her other hand. Not exotics, bought from any florist but flowers she had picked herself from the ground and the woods around the mill. Not to save money: she knew he must always have missed these.

Time to close the circle. As she stepped forward to the grave, Andy released her hand. Meg stood in front of the simple headstone, her head bowed and the silent tears streaming down her face.

Here lay a decent man, who had lived a decent life. Had loved, like any man, and maybe loved too much. Until that unrequited love had become an obsession which had shaped, and possibly ruined, his life.

A good man, who had won the respect of many. Yet he had been buried without so much as a friend to stand and mourn him, as Meg was now doing.

A man she had never known, but someone who had reached through the gates of Death to gift her the mill, and the chance to change every aspect of her life. The most powerful, wonderful act of human kindness she had ever experienced.

'Thank you, Henry,' she whispered. 'Thank you, with all my heart.'

She reached down, gently laying, then spreading, the small woodland flowers in a simple and colourful arc beneath the headstone.

'You *have* put it right,' she said unsteadily. 'Whatever it was that worried you, whatever wouldn't fade in the shadows of your mind. If you weren't my Dad, no father could have acted with more kindness than you showed. If you were my Dad, I only wish I could have met you, and got to know you better. What's past, is past. So rest in peace, my dear . . . '

The flowers blurred, as she felt Andy's hand slip gently over hers. No words spoken, just a silent presence at her side. As, she knew in her heart, he would always be — full of nonsense when the mood was on him, full of strength when that was what she needed most. As she did now.

Meg stepped back. 'Let's go,' she said quietly.

They walked slowly down the gravel path towards the cemetery gate, the unending rumble of London traffic sounding over everything from the roads outside. Maybe it was a state of mind, but the very air she breathed seemed second-hand.

As they reached Andy's travel-stained truck — the run would do it good, he had said — she turned and looked back. The cemetery seemed such a bleak place, the last place on earth where she would want to be buried herself. Part of her ached at the thought of leaving Henry here.

'We can always come back,' Andy said quietly. 'As often as it takes.'

'And if we don't come here again, ever?'

'Then it doesn't matter. What does is the memory of the man that you will keep in your heart. That's where he belongs, not here.'

'You're a philosopher, Andy,' she said, a catch in her voice.

'I'm a Yorkshireman,' he said broadly. 'Leave t' dead where they lie an' keep your worrying for the living.'

Meg smiled. 'Another ancient Yorkshire saying?' she asked.

'Nay, lass,' he smiled back. ''Tis but common sense.' He unlocked the door of his truck and looked around. Houses on every horizon, tall tower blocks and office buildings behind. No hill or green field within a day's walking. He shuddered. 'Ower many fowk here — both vertical an' horizontal. Let's go home.'

We do hope that you have enjoyed reading this large print book.

Did you know that all of our titles are available for purchase?

We publish a wide range of high quality large print books including:
Romances, Mysteries, Classics
General Fiction
Non Fiction and Westerns

Special interest titles available in large print are:
The Little Oxford Dictionary
Music Book
Song Book
Hymn Book
Service Book

Also available from us courtesy of Oxford University Press:
Young Readers' Dictionary
(large print edition)
Young Readers' Thesaurus
(large print edition)

For further information or a free brochure, please contact us at:
Ulverscroft Large Print Books Ltd.,
The Green, Bradgate Road, Anstey,
Leicester, LE7 7FU, England.
Tel: (00 44) 0116 236 4325
Fax: (00 44) 0116 234 0205

Other titles published by
The House of Ulverscroft:

THE VALLEY OF THE VINES

Mark Neilson

Sophie Hargreaves hopes to repair her shattered family by buying a rundown vineyard in Piedmont and bringing everyone together again. Sadly, her attempt fails and she's left struggling to bring in the grape harvest on her own before she faces ruin. Then, just as she begins to lose hope, Sophie finds help from an unlikely source: three strangers fleeing a storm and its flooding. They find themselves wrestling with the problems of saving the grapes and making the ancient winery viable. Unexpectedly, Sophie finds a new life in the remote wine valleys of Northern Italy.

DIARY OF A GRUMPY OLD GIT

Tim Collins

Dave Cross believed he was reasonably cheerful — until somebody bought him a 'Grumpy Old Git' diary in the office Secret Santa. Determined to prove them wrong, he resolves to be positive for an entire year. But it's not easy when your wife runs off with an estate agent and the new boss is young, ambitious and determined to make you actually do some work. Then there's the everyday horrors of public transport, shopping technology, popular culture and dating — a sunny outlook is asking too much. But with his fiftieth birthday looming, Dave is determined to make his life less shambolic . . .